A Zigzag Path

The following historical novels are also
by David Macpherson

Defenders of Mai-dun.
A story of the Roman invasion of Dorset

Nomad.
A story of the Tibetan Uprising

All Lies.
A Story of the Portland Spy Ring

The Black Box
A story of Monmouth's Rebellion
and the Bloody Assizes

Aquarius (pub in 2016)
A story of the building of the Dorchester Aqueduct

All are available through Amazon and Kindle

A Zigzag Path

A Story of Smuggling set in Weymouth and Portland

By

David Macpherson

PROLOGUE

4*th* June 1824   4 Brandy Row,
                                      Chesilton,
                                Isle of Portland,
                                         Dorset.

Dear Amanda and Beth,

Tom Verney paused, stared at what he had written, then screwed up the paper and threw it into a basket in the corner of the room. He reached for another sheet of paper and started again.

4*th* June 1824   4 Brandy Row,
                                      Chesilton,
                                Isle of Portland,
                                         Dorset.

My Dearest Sisters,

As I promised you, here is the first of what I hope will be regular letters. You will be pleased to hear that I am happy and well. Uncle Toby in Poole has indeed given me a job. I am appointed as a Riding Officer in the new Coast Guard Service. I am to be based in Weymouth, thirty miles from Poole. Uncle Toby has given me a sweet little pony called Augustus, though I call him Gussy. I will be paid the princely sum of £42 a year. I am afraid I will not have much money spare to send to you for a while. Just keeping myself alive will take most of my weekly wage.

My immediate employer is Captain Bouscarle, who is the chief excise officer for Weymouth. His title is Collector of Customs. He seems to be a very kind man, and I feel sure I can get on with him. There are no vacancies for Riding Officers in Weymouth and I think Captain Bouscarle is a little put out that Uncle Toby has foisted his godson on him. I don't expect any favours from him. He has found a billet for me at the above address on the Island of Portland, which you will see on your map of Dorset, is close by Weymouth. The other excise men in this division are stationed in Portland Castle, but I am told there is no room for me there for the moment.

No 4 Brandy Row, my cottage, has only two rooms in it, and was previously used as a fisherman's store. It is stoutly built of local stone with a thatched roof. Gussy is stabled in a shed at the rear. The cottage is at the top end of Brandy Row and overlooks Chesil Beach and the sea. I will have the constant swish of the waves on the pebbles to lull me to sleep. The very name 'Brandy Row' suggests that there are smugglers in the area and I expect to be kept busy in my work. Yesterday I went to have a drink in the taproom of The Cove House Inn, which is only a hundred yards from where I live, but I could find no one to talk to. I expect they are all a little suspicious of a customs officer.

Portland is not really an island, but I had to use a quaint old ferry from the mainland to get here. I am told there is a causeway, which horses and carts can use at low tide, but I haven't discovered it yet.

Tom carefully read through what he had written. The whole letter was a mixture of lies and half-truths, but he had no wish to unburden his misery onto his two young sisters. He decided to finish with at least one sentiment that was honest.

I hope you are both well and that Aunt Edith is looking after you properly. I think of you both constantly and am determined that soon we will be together again. Amanda, look after Bess and make sure she does her schoolwork. Bess, remember it is not easy for your sister to be in charge. Try to support her decisions.

Your loving brother,
Tom

Writing to his sisters made Tom sick with misery. His comfortable life had so recently been wrenched from him. Despite sensible Amanda's insistence he still felt guilt for his father's death and scared about his uncertain future.

Chapter 1
The Riding Officer

The series of events that led to Tom's present misery had started just as it was getting dark in late April. He had noticed a flickering light coming from the window of the church tower and had drawn his father's attention to this. The Reverend Daniel Verney, newly appointed vicar of St Mary's, Sixpenny Handley in the county of Dorset, though it necessary to investigate. 'Come over to the church with me Tom,' his father invited. 'You've had your nose buried in that book all afternoon and the fresh air will do you good.' But the boy was too engrossed in his new law book to accept and too wrapped up in himself to notice the concern in his father's request.

Twenty minutes later Amanda the elder of Tom's two sisters, capable and just a little bossy as any 16 year old who has run a household for the last three years is entitled to be, poked her head round the door. 'Tell Papa that supper is nearly ready,' she instructed Tom. With a start he realised his father had not returned from the church. He dragged himself from the comfort of his armchair, stretching the kinks from his body, and went to investigate. Though he was nearly 19 years old Tom was still spooked by the silence of the churchyard and his imagination raced as his flickering lantern dimly lit the path through the silent gravestones. The church door was half open but he could see no light from inside. There was no answer to his call of 'Father'. Unnerved he was turning to go back to the vicarage, hoping he would find his father there, when he saw a body lying in a pool of blood at the foot of the tower. He frantically searched for any sign of life, but a knife wound to the chest had brought to an end the career of a god-fearing man many had predicted one day would become a bishop.

Whispers among local people soon started to circulate that the vicar had surprised a gang of smugglers, who were using his church as a temporary storage space for contraband brandy casks. Sixpenny Handley had a long smuggling reputation. When the notorious Isaac Gulliver had lived in the village it had been a centre and transport hub for goods smuggled all along the Dorset coast. But the one time landlord of The King's Arms, had long since moved his base of operation nearer to the sandy beaches of Poole Harbour, before he acquired respectability and became one of the churchwardens of Wimborne Minster. Anyhow Isaac Gulliver had died two years earlier and it was said his gang had never intentionally killed anyone. Though the rumours about smuggling persisted, the constable arrested no one for the Reverend Verney's murder, and no evidence to indicate a likely killer was found.

On the day of the funeral Tom and his two younger sisters had received a curt note from the secretary to the Bishop of Salisbury telling them that they must be out of the vicarage by the middle of May, ten days away. The three had made a forlorn little group round the grave. The Reverend Verney had been inducted to his church only three weeks earlier and most of the villagers had no personal loyalty to him or his family. Many had themselves been involved over the years in smuggling operations and knew it safest not to show too much sympathy to the family. Daniel's unmarried sister, Miss Edith Verney, a stern and unsmiling woman, supported the children. She had offered to take the girls into her home in Salisbury. Also present was Captain Toby Fortescue, brother of the children's long dead mother. Besides being Tom's uncle and godfather, Captain Fortescue was also the commander of the newly formed Coast Guard Service in Poole. As a junior lieutenant on HMS Victory he had served under Captain Hardy and Admiral Nelson at Trafalgar. He had been promoted Captain just before the Peace of Paris had caused a serious reduction in the number of officers the Royal Navy required. Rather than fester on half-pay waiting for some opportunity to arise, Toby Fortescue had applied for a post in the Excise Service. When the new Coast Guard Service was formed in 1823 his old Captain, now Commodore Thomas Hardy had supported his promotion to the prestigious position of Commander of the Coast Guard in Poole.

Fortescue was an unimaginative and austere man who had never married. He had little experience with children and was happy to leave his nieces' fate to Edith Verney. At his brother-in-law's funeral, he did realise that he had some obligation to help Tom, his only nephew, and also his godson. 'You won't be going up to university now young man. Come down to Poole and I will see what I can do about finding you a place.' With that he left the graveside and stomped off to his horse, Tom presumed to return to Poole some 22 miles away.

Tom recognised his ambitions to take a place at Oxford were now in tatters. His capable sister Amanda had taken over the running of the household from the age of 13 on the death of their mother, allowing Tom to indulge himself in studying philosophy and law. He was neither unkind nor uncaring, just unused to taking decisions and at this moment he had no idea where to turn for help. His aunt Edith apologised that she would not be able to provide accommodation for him as well as his sisters, but did agree to house a few valuable pieces of furniture from the vicarage until Tom might, at some future date, require them. Six days after the funeral Tom paid a local carter his last silver coins to carry his sisters and some books and furniture the 14 miles to Salisbury. Amanda and Bess, bewildered and frightened at the sudden change in their fortune, clung to him as he kissed them goodbye. He promised he would come and see them as soon as circumstances allowed and also that he would write regularly. As he had no other idea what to do, he decided to take up his uncle's offer of 'a place.' He knew little about the sea and less about the Customs or Coast Guard Services, but he had no wish to stay in the unfriendly environment of Sixpenny Handley where any one of the villagers could have been his father's murderer. Like a latter day Dick Whittington, but without the cat and heading for Poole rather than London, he set off to find his fortune.

Toby Fortescue was not a very pleasant man, nor had his naval career been a sparkling success. By 1814 he was one of the oldest lieutenants in the royal navy as successive promotion boards had passed him over, guessing correctly that his unimaginative mind and grumpy manner would not be conducive to good discipline on any ship he captained. Commodore Hardy had only supported the cause of one of his previous junior officers because he could scarcely remember him. Fortescue hadn't expected his casual offer to Tom at the graveside to be taken up. When the boy presented himself at the Customs House in Poole, his immediate thought was how he could get rid of him with the minimum inconvenience to himself. Grudgingly he offered him a bed for the night. Next day he wrote to the Collector in Weymouth, Captain Jim Bouscarle, instructing him to find a position for his orphaned nephew. He also ordered one of his clerks to buy the cheapest horse he could find from the local gypsies and as soon as possible sent Tom off to report to Weymouth.

The first nineteen years of Tom's life had been remarkably uncomplicated. Despite the death of his mother when he was 16, he had been brought up in a cheerful and loving family. His father had provided a strong ethical framework for all his children as well as for his own life, for he was no hypocrite. The *Ten Commandments* were not some vague set of rules for lip service, but a moral code he expected his children to live by. His Christianity was an uncompromising religion, but none of his children ever felt either restricted by it or unloved by him. With his sudden death Tom felt he had lost his moral compass. The ungracious attitude of his uncle had shocked him. Toby Fortescue's meanness in buying an aging, spavined and undernourished pony, and the cheapest mount he could get away with, was a gesture he found difficult to understand. It was a sad and confused young man who plodded wearily towards Weymouth that afternoon. Every few miles Tom would dismount and walk for a while beside his exhausted horse. He had already shared his worries with Augustus, which he gathered was the animal's name. Augustus appeared to be a sympathetic listener. 'I'll call you Gussie,' he told him. 'The only Augustus I know was the first Roman emperor, and to be honest, you don't look very imperial to me. The two of them plodded on. 'We make a pathetic pair,' he later confided to Gussie, who looked as if he wanted to drop dead rather than drag one more hoof in front of the other. 'I would prefer to be anywhere in England rather than travelling to meet the unknown Captain Bouscarle. If he's anything like my uncle, I'll not be staying, Gussie, I promise you. We'll turn round and head off as far from the coast as we can.' Gussie looked at him with mournful eyes saying nothing.

Tom was directed to the Custom House on the quay in Weymouth harbour. Captain Jim Bouscarle, Collector of Customs for Weymouth, Portland and Wyke, looked up from the report he was writing as Tom entered the office. He accepted the letter that Tom held out to him and read it in silence. He looked almost as tired and dispirited as Gussie. Whatever Acts of Parliament were promulgated from London to establish the new Coast Guard Service nothing effective would happen unless The Service was adequately funded. The Weymouth Excise Office was now supposed to collect all customs dues from ships arriving at the port, to arrange for patrols along the coast from Abbotsbury to Lulworth in order to prevent smuggling and to provide a rescue service for ships in distress whenever necessary. Jim Bouscarle did not need an extra Riding Officer, he needed money to pay those already employed. 'Your uncle wants me to give you a job,' he said as he finished reading. 'Do you have a horse?'

Now was not the time to deny Augustus his birthright. 'Yes sir. He's tied up outside.' Tom looked out of the window. He could just see Gussie leaning tiredly against the Customs House wall. He hoped he would still have a live horse by the time the interview was over.

Captain Bouscarle called for his clerk. 'Arthur. This is Mr Verney. Find somewhere for him to spend the night here in Weymouth, then tomorrow send him over to join Overton and the other officers at Portland Castle.' He would shuffle the problem of what to do with Tom down the line to his second in command. He felt a slight twinge of conscience. Saul Overton was not a very pleasant man and the Captain suspected not an honest one. He was constantly complaining about the standard of accommodation in Portland Castle and would not welcome another member to his team. This would not be an ideal training post for a young toff still wet behind the ears. Under Saul's tutelage Tom would either sink or swim. If the smugglers didn't sort him out then the brutal lieutenant, who had scant respect for the gentry, probably would. He scribbled a brief note for Tom to hand on to Overton and rising from his chair he shook Tom's hand. 'Welcome to the Service. I'm dining with the military at the barracks tonight, so I regret I cannot entertain you. Arthur is Comptroller here. He will look after you.' He looked vaguely round his office and with a casual wave he left.

'The Captain doesn't bother himself with details,' the little clerk said. 'He leaves all that sort of stuff to me.' Arthur was one of the smallest men Tom had ever seen. His rat-like face and scheming eyes suggested to Tom that the man would find many opportunities to use 'the details' to his own advantage. His next words confirmed that suspicion. 'You see me right, Mr Verney, and I'll look after you.'

Tom wondered if he was expected to give Arthur some money right away as a bribe or tip. If so, he was going to be disappointed. 'I'm sorry. I don't have any money at present. I had hoped that Captain Bouscarle would advance me some of my first month's salary so I could get myself settled in.'

'Don't fret yourself, boy.' Arthur patted him on the shoulder. Far from being reassuring, this unctuous manner turned Tom's stomach. 'I'll find food for you tonight at the Black Dog and you can sleep here in the office. There's a spare mattress in the storeroom. Tomorrow we will arrange for Mrs Givens to make your uniform. The cost of that will be taken from your first month's pay. I'll make sure you have sufficient funds to buy your commons until next payday, so you'll not starve. As I told you, Arthur will see you right.'

The Black Dog was a dingy public house over the river from the Customs House. Even though the sun had yet to set beyond the harbour, little light penetrated through the grimy panes of glass that filled the window frames. The atmosphere was heavy with tobacco smoke and stale beer. Tom nervously followed as closely as he could, behind his tiny companion, as he pushed his way between the long, wooden tables. Peering through the smoke he noticed several games of dominoes and backgammon were in progress, but most of the players had temporarily stopped to take notice of the new arrivals. The clerk was obviously well known to the rough clientele of the bar room. 'Who's the young pup Arthur?' a coarse voice called out.

'New bluebottle; going to join Overton on Portland.' Arthur shouted over his shoulder. He grabbed at Tom's arm and dragged him past the fireplace and through a doorway into the snug. There was an empty table in the corner and the two of them sat down on a low pine bench facing the kitchen.

Tom was beginning to wonder if he had been wise to let the clerk look after him, but with no money or alternative accommodation he had little option and he was very hungry. At least someone was taking the necessary decisions for him. He looked round the room at the other occupants who sat at their tables in an uneasy silence. Eventually a burly man, Tom guessed was the innkeeper, came out of the kitchen and approached them. 'Who's this, Arthur?'

The clerk struggled to his feet dragging Tom after him. 'Nathan, this is Mr Tom Verney the new Riding Officer for Portland. Tom, this is Mr Nathan Raditch, landlord of The Black Dog.' The innkeeper was a man who looked as if he could more than hold his own in a fight. Tom suspected that any drunkards in the house would not last long should they be a nuisance to Mr Raditch. His sturdy frame, his long black hair tied in a ponytail, bushy black eyebrows and full black beard gave him a piratical aspect. Tom held out his hand and Raditch, first wiping his own on a grimy apron, took it in a firm grip.

'Mr Verney has no money and I hoped you would consider giving him a bowl of your potage as this is his first day.' Tom had not expected that he would need to ask for charity and was embarrassed by his position. He was also conscious that Arthur now seemed not quite as confident as he had appeared on entering The Black Dog. The innkeeper was obviously not a close friend…perhaps more of a business acquaintance.

'Mr Verney is welcome to eat here Arthur,' Raditch said. 'I expect we shall do business in the future.' He turned on his heel and walked back to the kitchen.

Arthur let out a deep breath and seemed to relax. Tom vaguely wondered what sort of business a Riding Officer and an innkeeper might conduct in the future, but he kept his thoughts to himself and was soon rewarded for his silence by a steaming bowl of fish chowder accompanied by a hunk of bread. This was the first food he had eaten since he had left Poole that morning.

Arthur ordered two mugs of brandy mixed with water. As soon as these were placed in front of them the other customers resumed their whispered conversations. 'Good health,' Arthur said raising his mug. 'This'll keep the cold out tonight, though I doubt the keg it came from ever saw the King's mark on it.' If Tom thought that The Black Dog was hardly a suitable place for the Weymouth Comptroller of Excise to be drinking, he sensibly kept quiet about it.

Chapter 2
A Rough Welcome

Tom had hoped that his new life was going to be the sort of adventure that he could, on some future occasion, retell to his sisters with exciting details of the camaraderie between fellow officers as they bravely tried to enforce the King's law. Instead, all he had to show for four days in the Coast Guard Service was a grimy upper room in a broken down cottage with a straw mattress in the corner and a dirty rug loaned to him by the one half-decent person he had met since he had left Sixpenny Handley. He admitted to himself that Captain Bouscarle had been honourable, but even the inexperienced Tom could recognise that he was a weak man who was overwhelmed by the scope of the work he was expected to do.

The morning after he had left the customs house and the objectionable Arthur, he had ridden Gussie, partially reinvigorated by his night's sleep, along the beach from Weymouth to the spur of shingle that stretched out from the small village of Wyke. From there Tom made his way to the ferry crossing to Portland, where the lagoon known as the Fleet emptied into Portland Roads and Weymouth Bay. Arthur had explained to him that as a king's officer he was entitled to free passage every time he used the ferry. Portland was a royal manor owned by the king and the crown's representatives on the island ran the ferry service from Wyke.

He found the ancient ferryman puffing on a pipe inside the ramshackle hut that Arthur had grandly called the ferryman's cottage. At first he had refused Tom's request for a free passage. 'King's Officers wears uniform,' Tom was curtly informed. 'That's how I knows they be King's Officers.' But when Tom had explained his position, the ferryman had reluctantly agreed to transport Tom and Gussie to the other side. There were two ferries, small flat-bottomed barges, attached to wooden piles driven into the shingle. Tom wondered why the ferryman had decided laboriously to pull the boat from the Portland side over to the Wyke beach when there was a perfectly good ferry right by them. 'This'n's for folk. T'other'n for beasts. You and the nag must go in the boat for beasts.'

As the second ferry crunched on the pebbles Tom could see that this was indeed much the grimier of the two and this one had nowhere for him to sit down. He led Gussie to the water's edge, then gingerly along a short gangplank and down into the well of the boat. The ferryman grabbed hold of the rope and hand over hand pulled the ungainly craft across the tide, which by now was rushing out of the Fleet lagoon. There was no conversation between the two of them and as the boat crunched onto the Portland beach the ferryman lowered the gangplank back in position and watched as Tom led Gussie onto dry land. Then, without a word, he started pulling his ferry back towards the mainland.

Tom could see the impressive Portland Castle on the island's north shore about two miles to his left. To reach this from the ferry at Smallmouth, he and

Gussie had to walk along a narrow sandy causeway, riddled with rabbit warrens, called Coneygar Bank. This bank separated the shallow, tidal flatlands of the Mere from Portland Roadstead. His orders from Captain Bouscarle were to report to Saul Overton at Portland Castle.

On closer inspection the castle looked far less magnificent than it had from a distance. The pale stonework appeared to be crumbling and one of the gates was hanging drunkenly off its hinges. A listless guard, dressed in the blue and white uniform of the Royal Regiment of Engineers, was picking his nose as he leant against one of the stone pillars of the gatehouse. He showed no interest in Tom or Gussie or their authorisation to enter the castle. Anxious not to make a poor first impression Tom decided to dismount before passing through the gateway. He was aware that Gussie might do something foolish like stumbling, fouling or falling down dead. Once inside the courtyard he became aware of an officer, whom he rightly assumed would be Lieutenant Overton, lounging on a bench against the castle wall. Overton was watching a man scrubbing clothes by the pump. Tom handed over Captain Bouscarle's letter and stood anxiously while Overton read it without comment. The sun beat down on the courtyard and Tom, waiting to be welcomed by the Lieutenant, looked round at his future accommodation

Lieutenant Overton continued to sit in silence and his lack of any reaction made Tom nervous. He was anxious to start off on the right footing with the man who, after all, was now his commanding officer. 'Captain Fortescue in Poole is my godfather,' he blurted out. 'He promised to give me a job when my father was killed.'

'Well, now. So you're the Captain's little chum are you?' Overton asked with a sneer. 'Why aren't you in uniform? Expecting special treatment are you just because you've relatives in high places? Let me see.' He paused, apparently deep in thought, 'I believe the set of rooms we usually give to important visitors is taken for the season.'

His sarcasm was lost on Tom who had never come across instantaneous hatred before. 'My uniform is still being made by Mrs Givens,' he stammered. 'She said it should be ready in three days. As for accommodation, I don't want anything special. A simple room will be fine, honestly.' His voice tailed off as he waited to see how his answer would be received

Lieutenant Overton stood up from the seat. He had been supervising the young man washing clothes, now he was prepared to enjoy himself. Though Tom was nearly six foot tall, Overton towered over him. His trousers Tom recognised as part of a revenue officer's uniform, but the Lieutenant had discarded his jacket and shirt and stood in vest and braces appraising Tom. 'Come here Dawkins,' he called out. The youth, not much older than Tom, left the pump and hurried over. 'Dawkins. This is Riding Officer Verney, latest recruit to our happy little band. A single room for his accommodation will serve him fine. Where shall we put him?' Hugh Dawkins was no stranger to Overton's sarcasm and bullying. He was relieved that it was not he this time that was the butt of Overton's mockery. He felt a deal of sympathy for Tom, but was careful not to show it.

'Not much room in the Gunners' Quarters,' he mumbled keeping his eyes lowered.

'Indeed. For once in his futile life, Riding Officer Dawkins is correct.' How Saul Overton loved making these pompous pronouncements to anyone and everyone. 'There is no room even for a skinny little vermin like you Verney. Verney the vermin; I like the sound of that.' His smile had little humour in it. His narrow eyes and heavy features suggested cunning rather than intelligence. Tom felt scared but was determined not to show it. He could do little except stand there and take whatever cheap jibes Overton had to offer. He would have liked to be anywhere but the courtyard of Portland Castle, but his life was so bleak at present there was nowhere else for him to go.

'Well, Vermin, as Dawkins here says there is no room in the castle for you to plant your scrawny arse. You will have to lodge in the fisherman's cottage in Chesilton. You know it Dawkins? The one we confiscated from the local criminals at the top of Brandy Row. Until you get your uniform you can't stand duty as a Riding Officer, so you'd better take the time to get to know our little island. Talk to the cretins who live here and learn all the likely coves for landing. When you're properly dressed report back here and you can start doing your job.' He quickly lost interest in the two young men and turned away to walk into a low building on the right that was linked to the gatehouse. He stopped in the doorway and stood looking at them as if daring either of them to speak. 'Take him over to Chesilton as soon as you've finished my clothes Dawkins.' He turned away and closed the door behind him.

There was an awkward pause which Tom ended by asking, 'Why are you washing his clothes?'

'All of us do whatever Lieutenant Overton tells us.' Dawkins moved back towards the pump and started to rinse the clothes. Tom went with him, noticing that on the far edge of the yard they would be out of earshot from the lieutenant's lodgings. 'My name is Hugh.' He offered his hand to Tom. 'We've learned it isn't worth it to refuse. When I first came here I told him I wasn't going to polish his kit when he asked me to. That resulted in a string of all the worst duties the following week and my pay mysteriously being delayed at the end of the month. Nothing too obvious, but when I offered to do his boots for him, the duty rota immediately changed and my pay turned up. I got the message. We all find it's easier to do what he wants.' He paused to wring out one of the shirts he had been rinsing and Tom waited for him to continue. 'The devil is certainly cunning. His requests are never so unreasonable that it is worth making a complaint, but every time you do what he asks, his control over you tightens just that little bit more. He is truly a horrid man.'

'I think, with bullies, the only way to deal them is to stand up to them.' Even as he spoke Tom realised how pompous his words sounded. 'I mean...,' he hesitated. 'surely, if we all work together we can convince him...,' he tailed off and Hugh didn't even bother to answer him.

When Hugh had finished laying out Overton's clothes to dry on a low stone wall, he offered to show

Tom around. 'As well as four of us customs men, there are fifteen soldiers from the artillery reserve living in the castle and one officer, Lieutenant Hendrick. He and Overton have the Master Gunner's Quarters, which is where he has just gone. The soldiers are supposed to be here to man the guns in an emergency. They keep themselves to themselves, but revenue officers can call on them for help. Mostly they just sit around doing nothing.' The two young men entered the castle by a zigzag passage through the twelve-foot thick walls into a large room. 'This is Garrison Hall where all of us eat,' Hugh explained. The long thin space, dimly lit by narrow slit windows, was littered with bits of food and dirty straw. 'Riding Officers sleep in the next room which used to be the gunner's quarters.' He led Tom into another dingy little space on the left of the hall. A tired old man looked up from a cot in one corner. 'Matthew, this is Tom Verney, who's come to join us.' Matthew said nothing and turned over on his mattress. 'He's a bit deaf,' Hugh whispered, 'and doesn't do much which suits Overton perfectly.' Tom hoped Hugh Dawkins might become a friend, but there was little sparkle in this downtrodden young man. He wondered what Hugh had meant by his last remark. *No doubt I'll find out in time*, he thought.

'The only other Riding Officer is Henry Drake. He's married and older than us. He works in a draper's shop in Wakeham where his family lives. Overton makes him sleep here every night when he's not on watch, so he doesn't see much of his children.' Tom thought he could have found room for a mattress on the floor if necessary, or the Lieutenant could have made room for him by allowing Drake to sleep at home, but decided to say nothing. Perhaps he would be better off in the fisherman's cottage Overton had mentioned. The residents of the castle did not seem a particularly happy bunch.

Hugh let Tom into another room, which was dominated by five huge cannons aiming through the gaps in the walls out to sea. He pointed at a row of wooden cubicles against the inside wall. 'This is where the soldiers sleep. It's called the Gun Room. I 'spect you can guess why.'

The two young men peered out of one of the gunports looking at Portland Harbour below. 'Come down to the quay and see the *Samphire.*' At the mention of *Samphire* Hugh showed his first flash of enthusiasm and Tom followed him out of the castle and down some steps to the quay. *Samphire* turned out to be a smart revenue cutter tied up next to the castle's water gate. 'Lieutenant Overton is the only one who takes her out,' Hugh explained. 'He has two or three crewmen who work in the Mermaid pub here in Castletown. He won't let any of the Riding Officer's go out with him. They stood admiring the little craft and Tom asked about the two small cannons, which nestled in the well of the boat. 'Those are three-pounders,' Hugh told him. 'We aren't given much gunpowder to use so they've never been fired while I have been stationed here. They wouldn't be much good against a smuggler's boat of any size say a lugger or a brig, but they could certainly sink a local fishing boat. If we need something bigger we send to Weymouth for the *Georgia.* She's a lugger with a crew of nine, but neither boat ever seems to catch any smugglers.'

Tom admitted he knew little about sailing and Hugh happily explained that *Samphire* was gaff rigged with two headsails and a fair turn of speed. He obviously loved sailing and shyly admitted it has his ambition to command one of the revenue boats. 'So far Lieutenant Overton has always said no when I have asked if I can go out with him.'

At Hugh's suggestion they collected a blanket and an old kettle from the storeroom and some basic supplies from the castle kitchen before they set off for Chesilton. Hugh apologetically explained that his welsh cob, Lucretia, was a little too old for the work on the island, but to Tom she looked like a Derby winner compared with Gussie. As they drew away from the castle and the influence of Lieutenant Overton, Tom saw Hugh becoming gradually more relaxed. The two chatted easily and Tom began to learn about the work of a Riding Officer. 'We often have to go out at night, as that is when the smugglers try to land their contraband. Some people call them 'Gentlemen of the Night,' but the only free traders I have come across have been Portland fishermen trying to earn a bit of cash to stay alive. Most of the people on the island are involved in the trade in one way or another, but we don't have any of the big sharks on Portland. Last month we brought three fishermen before the court in Weymouth. They claimed they had found some barrels of brandy floating in the sea off Chesil Beach. The magistrates fined them ten shillings each. That's probably less than they would have earned as profit from selling each barrel. Somehow the smugglers always seem to avoid our patrols, so we don't get much action. I suppose it makes a difference just being seen around.' They jogged along in silence for a few minutes. 'Governor Penn is in charge on the island. I'm sure he could put a stop to smuggling if he really wanted to,' Hugh said. 'Actually I don't see what harm it does and the people on the island are really poor. Without a little smuggling they probably couldn't survive.'

'But it is against the law,' Tom said. Once again even to himself this sounded unnecessarily pompous and he was not surprised that Hugh didn't reply.

The village of Chiswell or Chesilton as the locals called it was a scattered collection of stone houses and cottages under the lea of the huge pebble bank called Chesil Beach. 'Chesil is the old Dorset word for a pebble,' Hugh explained. 'These people are mainly fishermen.' Tom noticed the collection of boats pulled up on the beach out of reach of the waves with crab pots and nets hanging from every post and rail outside the houses. Some scruffy children were playing ball on a worn piece of grass and it was they who directed Hugh and Tom up the hill when they asked for Brandy Row.

No 4 was a tiny broken down little cottage at the top of the village next to the sea. The front door had been broken off its hinges by some previous violent entry and now two planks of wood roughly nailed to the frame held it in place. The thatched roof looked old and sodden. Hugh suggested that they should tie their horses up round the back and there they found a lean-to shed which could act as a stable for Gussie. When Tom had levered off the planks and eased open the remains of the front door the two young men entered. The downstairs had obviously been used as a storeroom. Against one wall there was a fireplace full of junk and a small area next to it that could be used as a kitchen. The single window was filthy, but the glass appeared to be intact. Piles of old netting and the inevitable lobster and crab pots were strewn around. In the far corner, a sturdy ladder led to a hatch in the ceiling. Tom lifted the hatch and looked at the room that was for the time being to become his home. Again he was relieved to see that the glass was intact in the window though he could see cracks of daylight between the window frame and the stonework. The whole room was extremely dusty but appeared to be dry. A pile of straw in one corner, Tom decided, was likely to be his bed that night. Hugh followed Tom up the steps and the two of them stood surveying the room. 'At least you've got the single accommodation you asked for,' Hugh said with a grin.

On the afternoon ride over from the castle Hugh had again and again shown his determination to see things in the best possible light. Never was his optimism more desperately needed. 'There are four hours before I am needed back in the castle. Let's see if we can make this a little more homely. I'll try to borrow a broom and bucket from one of your neighbours. You bring upstairs the stuff we collected from the castle.' Together they set about the dirt, though Hugh's efforts with the borrowed broom seemed to generate rather than remove the accumulate dust. After a couple of hours hard graft the upstairs room had a reasonable resemblance to a living space. Some old newsprint had been stuffed into the cracks in the window frame and one of the boxes they discovered in the storeroom had been brought upstairs for use as a table. Tom had found an ancient oil lamp in the shed around the back, which he had optimistically cleaned up and was confident it could be made to work with the appropriate wick and fuel. Pleased with their efforts Hugh suggested that the two of them should have a drink in The Cove House Inn to cement their new friendship before he had to ride back to the castle.

Chapter 3
Fishing

The first sound Tom heard when he woke, as it had been the last sound before he went to sleep, was that of the waves crashing on the beach close to his front door. This boom was followed by a deep rumble as the surf dragged back the pebbles with its vicious undertow. He lay on his straw mattress looking out from the low attic window as the early morning sun flecked the tops of the waves. It was going to be fine again and he had three days of freedom before he had to report back to Lieutenant Overton. If he were to make a success of his new job, and despite the setbacks of the last two days this he was determined to do, he would have to get to know the people and place he was to work with. After his conversations with Hugh the previous day he was aware that one of his greatest deficiencies was his almost complete ignorance of all matters to do with the sea, a sorry lack in a customs officer.

After a sad breakfast of some rather stale bread washed down by black tea, Tom led Gussie out onto the grassy area of the Underhill where the Portland sheep revelled in the rich maritime grass and the plentiful water that ran through the jumble of rocks known as the West Weare. He tied Gussie to a bush with the long piece of rope he had collected from the beach and left him, among the flocks on the pasture, contentedly munching away.

Satisfied that Gussie would come to no harm he returned to Brandy Lane and decided to explore the pebble bank called Chesil Beach. Later he was to discover that this was a feature unique in England. It stretched for 14 miles along the coast separated from the mainland for much of that distance by the Fleet lagoon. Over the centuries the sea had carefully graded the pebbles with the largest just outside Tom's cottage being the size of an orange to the smallest at West Bay being the size of a pea.

Laid out on the beach above the high water mark were eight or nine rowing boats several of them covered with fishing nets drying in the sun. Tom scrunched over the pebbles to inspect the nearest one. Built of wood and 18 feet in length it appeared to Tom to have a bow at each end. There were three pairs of thole pins on each side, which he guessed were to hold the oars secure and these, ten feet of beautiful white ash wood, were laid across the thwarts.

'That'll be my boat.'

Tom turned and saw an old man sitting on an upturned lobster creel puffing on a long clay pipe. 'Excuse me.' He walked over towards the man who was on the edge of the beach in front of the Cove House Inn.

'That'll be my boat you be lookin' at.'

'I'm sorry,' Tom said. 'I was interested. These boats. I have never seen anything like them before.'

'They be Portland lerrets, the finest fishing boat ever made. They be built here on the island and have never been known to tip over.' Tom introduced himself, but the grizzled fisherman refused his hand. 'I know who you be. You're the new Preventy living in Daniel's cottage.' He puffed away on his pipe while Tom stood wondering how to continue the conversation. 'I'm Samuel Ditchburn,' the old man swung round to look at Tom. 'I've fished here nigh on 60 years.'

Tom thought he looked far too ancient to be still fishing, but he was too tactful to say so to this scowling, reticent man. How do they…,' he stopped and thought of a better way to pose his question. 'How do you catch fish in a lerret?'

'By shooting the seine.' As Tom had no idea what this meant he was just about to ask what he suspected would be another stupid question when Samuel interrupted. 'If you wait around for some minutes you will see my boat taken out. That'll be useful for your learning.'

Tom certainly had nothing better to do and as Samuel was the first Portlander to speak to him, this seemed an ideal opportunity to find out something about the island. 'What makes the lerret so ideal for fishing?' he asked.

'Never been known to capsize, even in the roughest of seas.' As Tom had provided the old man with an ear for listening it was obvious that Sam Ditchburn was not going to waste the chance of a willing audience. 'London tried to give us one of those new fancy lifeboats with buoyancy fastened beneath the thwarts, but the lads would have none of it. They take the lerret out in almost any seas. It's only at the top of a gale that we can't launch.' While he was speaking a number of fisherman scrunched across the pebbles to the boat. Each of them acknowledged Samuel with a brief 'Morning Sam', and ignored Tom completely.

'What are they going to catch?' Tom asked.

'Spring and summer its mackerel, autumn it be sprats and in the winter mostly whiting. I guess today it'll be mackerel.' While the old man was talking Tom noticed that the jumble of men were forming themselves into some sort of order. 'Do you think I can help?' he asked.

'Nay, lad. You'd be a darned nuisance out there. Watch and learn. I 'spect they'll take only four oars today there being little enough wind.' As he spoke Tom saw four of the men climb into the boats and fix their oars between the thole pins. Another carefully folded a bundle of netting into the space in front of the rowers and four or five more gathered round the stern. 'Watch coxie now. He's spotting the wave.' As he spoke the coxswain dropped his hand and shouted at the shore party who rushed the boat down the pebbles into the waves. As the boat hit the water each of the rowers pulled on their oar and the coxswain nipped athletically over the stern into the boat. The lerret staggered as it hit the first of the waves but the momentum, established by those on shore and carried forward by the rowers, drove it through into calmer water. Tom noticed that the shore crew had kept hold of one end of a rope and had started to walk slowly up the beach as the coxswain carefully fed the seine net over the side.

'One edge of the seine be corked, t'other is weighted with stones from the beach,' Sam explained, as the lerret carved a graceful arc away from the shore. Fifteen minutes later the boat scrunched back on the pebbles and the rowers jumped out and began to haul on the ship-end rope. The shore party and the boat party met and together pulled in their respective ropes. Tom could see the line of corks bobbing in the waves and Sam, who seemed as excited this time as if he was a 14-year-old on his first fishing, beckoned him forward towards the sea. The men strained at the ropes as the net became heavier as it edged ashore. 'How can the men pull such a weight of net and fish onto the beach?' he asked Sam.

'They use the dip-nets leaving the seine in the water,' he was told. Sure enough while one of the fishermen secured both ends of the net to a stake driven into the pebbles the others waded into the sea and, dipping into the seine with small hand held nets, drew out the silver fish tipping them into wicker baskets. These were rushed up the pebble bank and emptied into holes scooped out above the tide line. Tom reckoned that the whole operation had taken just over an hour. 'Now you'll see why the Portland lerret has two bows,' Sam said with a chuckle. 'It'll make scant difference in a light wind like today, but in heavy seas if you try to turn a boat aside the wind she'll broach too and sink.' While he was talking, the oars were laid on the pebbles parallel to the sea and the boat, which was floating free beyond the waves, was carefully manoeuvred until it was opposite these makeshift rollers. Then after another shout from the coxswain both crews pulled on the bow rope and the lerret hit the shore and was rushed up the pebble bank until it too was clear of the high tide.

Sam walked over to the fishermen who seemed relaxed and cheerful after their successful morning. He picked two mackerel out from one of the pebble pits and handed them to Tom. 'These'll do for your tea lad. Best be off now.'

None of the other men had spoken to Tom and he guessed from Sam's remark that his presence was no longer welcome on the beach. He thanked Sam for the fish, and this was acknowledged with a raised hand. Tom made his way slowly back to No 4 Brandy Lane. He realised the truth of Sam's earlier remark: there was little he could have done to help such an expert display.

Next day Tom set out with Gussie to explore the island. Together they climbed the steep hill from Chiswell onto the upper plateau known as Tophill and wandered along the cliff path to the south. They passed the lookout rock called Tout that, Hugh had already told him, was a usual place for the smugglers to place a guard. The lookout would keep and eye not only on the ships in Lyme Bay, but also on the movement of the Riding Officers. The sun was shining and the coves and bays of the west coast looked very unsuitable for landing contraband. His four-mile journey to Portland Bill reminded Tom of the Sunday walks with his sisters before their tragic move to Dorset. At the southern tip of the island he scrambled to the top of Pulpit Rock wishing that Amanda and Beth could be with him. Spirited Beth would have been close behind him on the climb to the top. Amanda would have worried that she might fall, but would have screwed up her courage and been determined to follow them up. Looking back on the previous days Tom hoped that he would get to know Hugh Dawkins better and that he would become a proper friend. He was pleased to have chatted to Sam Ditchburn but knew that one old man was not the companionship he wanted. He was lonely.

Tom and Gussie returned home by the east of the island. The comparatively sheltered coves and the rickety piers jutting from the rocky esplanades looked much more promising sites for smugglers to land goods. Nearing an area known as Verne Yeates, just above Chiswell, he heard the sound of hammering. Peering over the edge of a vast pit he could see the quarrymen moving around like ants at the bottom of a deep hole. For over an hour Tom lay on the grass watching the intricate movements as the huge slabs of limestone were levered from the rock face, and dragged to the edge of the pit there to be jacked onto carts. He followed one cartload of stone, two horses in front and two at the rear, as the stone was manoeuvred down to the pier. The hind horses were dragged on their haunches as they braked the cart on the steep descent. Tom was appalled at such cruelty but was quickly coming to realise that life on Portland was tough, and so were the inhabitants. Next day he would collect his uniform and become a full Riding Officer of the Coast Guard Service.

Chapter 4
A Rough Start

That's enough sightseeing, thought Tom. *It's time I got down to some work.* He decided to set off for Weymouth early next morning. He needed to see Mrs Givens and collect his uniform. The taciturn ferryman answered his shout and hauled the 'ferry for beasts' over for him and Gussie.

'At bottom tide you can walk your horse across on the sand bar,' the man explained to Tom pointing out the shadowy spit of gravel just below the surface, which ran at an angle from the beach at Wyke. *He wouldn't have told me that if I had been paying a fare*, thought Tom.

Mrs Givens fussed over the fitting but had made an excellent job over his uniform. 'Make sure you keep it dry dear,' she told Tom. He admired himself in her mirror and thought he made quite a dashing figure in the navy blue jacket and trousers. He visited the Customs House and reported to Captain Bouscarle who seemed surprised to learn that he was not staying in the castle. Tom persuaded him that he needed another advance on his salary if he was to survive until the end of the month. The reluctant Arthur handed him another five guineas. By lunchtime he was ready to return to Portland. The ferryman showed a trifle more respect to his uniform but this was not true when he returned to Chesilton. He was surprised and a little hurt that the atmosphere of suspicion, something he had noticed on his first day on the island, had returned. The women and children either turned their backs on him or ignored him altogether as he and Gussie rode up Brandy Row.

In the evening Tom went for a walk on Tophill and ended up once again at Tout Rock. He sat down in the evening sunshine. He was not naturally introspective, but he began to reflect on his position. He had made one friend in Hugh, and a possible enemy of Lieutenant Overton, though he couldn't work out why. It was obvious that as a Riding Officer he was not welcome in Chesilton, where only Samuel Ditchburn had so far spoken to him, but this he could understand. A community where he was told many were involved with smuggling was hardly likely to welcome an officer of the customs service living amongst them. He was still determined to do his duty though he was beginning to feel rather on his own. Already he suspected that not all his fellow officers were as conscientious as he was.

While he was reviewing his life on the island, he idly noticed a two-masted lugger round Portland Bill and sail into Lyme Bay. In the light evening breeze she had a full set of sails and was gently drifting westwards across the wind towards Bridport. Even to Tom's inexperienced eye the captain seemed to know what he was doing. The ship went about smoothly and moved out to sea again on the starboard tack. She had no flag flying at the stern. Fifteen minutes later and the lugger completed a second circuit. *I wonder what the captain is waiting for,* Tom thought. *It'll be night soon. Why hasn't he made for harbour?*

A third circuit after fifteen more minutes convinced Tom that the captain was waiting for dark and his purpose was unlawful. He decided to go across to the castle and ask for advice. It didn't take him long, following the quarrymen's track down Verne Hill, to reach the castle. Hugh was alone in the hall. 'Where are the others?' Tom asked him, surprised at the quiet.

'Lieutenant Overton sent Matthew to watch Freshwater Bay and Henry's at Little Beach near The Grove. If they see anything suspicious they are to send for Lieutenant Hendrick who is patrolling the East Weares with his militiamen. Overton told us he had a tip off that there will be a landing tonight. He has sailed in *Samphire* and, according to Matthew, he has sent a warning to Captain Bouscarle asking him to take out the *Georgia* into Weymouth Bay if needed. And I'm stuck in this bloody castle missing all the fun. "You Dawkins will man the fort and act as communication centre," he said mimicking Overton's coarse voice.

'Overton's got it all wrong,' Tom said excited. 'It's not Weymouth Bay they're coming to, it's Lyme Bay.' He told Hugh about the two-master he had seen idling off Chesil Beach. 'The two of us could go and take a look. I am sure Overton would be pleased if we used our initiative and saved the Revenue Service the embarrassment of a total disaster.

'I dunno,' Hugh said worried. 'He did order me to stay here. You know he can be a right bastard if anyone crosses him. He tends to come down heavily on anyone who uses their initiative.'

'It's under half an hour to Chesil. You can be there and back before anyone knows you've gone.' Tom worked on a reluctant Hugh and eventually persuaded him that there was not much risk in a little private enterprise.

It was dark enough when they crawled into position just below the top of the pebble bank. The shadowy lugger was anchored a hundred yards off the beach, bare-masted and silent. Hugh pointed out the village of Fleet with its tiny church. 'That lot are well known to be at the heart of smuggling,' he whispered to Tom. 'Let me tell you something about smuggling. Somewhere near here must be the lander...he's in charge of the tubmen who make up the beach party.' As he spoke a light flashed three timers on the lugger. 'The lander will signal back that everything is all right,' Hugh said with all his experience of three months in the customs service. Neither of the boys could see any response from the shore and after a few minutes the light from the lugger flashed again. 'Shall I go back to the castle and let Lieutenant Overton know?' Hugh whispered.

Tom thought for a moment. 'Better hang on for a bit.' If there is no one on shore the lugger will probably sail off back to France and we will look pretty stupid. I wonder if our Dorset smugglers are on the other side of the island where Overton said the landing would happen.'

The two boys lay silently on the pebbles still warm from the summer sun, waiting to see what might happen next. Tom felt secure enough wrapped in the dark of the night when he heard the splash of oars followed by the crunch of a small boat onto the beach. Someone cursed in French and a lantern was again flashed briefly. Tom could just make out three or four men carrying small barrels up the beach to stack them above the tide mark less than fifty yards from where the boys lay.

'Don't think there's much we can do,' Hugh whispered. 'They're probably armed and there are more of them. We had better lie quiet until they have gone. I hope that won't be too long.' The little boat pushed off from the beach and returned to the lugger leaving the barrels stacked on the shingle. Tom and Hugh were just about to make a move when they heard once more the splash, splash of oars and once more the sound of a boat grounding. A second consignment of barrels were unloaded and carried up the beach. Ten minutes later a third followed by a fourth load were stacked alongside the original pile. 'The moon will be up soon,' Hugh whispered. 'I expect they will want to be away before then.' They could hear a muttered conversation but were too far away to hear what was said.

Eventually, 'Bonne chance.'

'That means good luck,' Tom whispered. One of the figures detached himself from the group and scrambled to the top of the pebble bank and began to walk down the other side. Tom could hear the man splashing his way across the Fleet lagoon while the rest of the party returned to their small craft and rowed back to the lugger. A few minutes later as the crescent moon rose slowly over Portland both boys could make out the sails of the lugger being unfurled and the ship slipping silently out to sea.

'Let's see what they have landed,' Hugh said, and together they crept as quietly as the pebbles would allow over to the stack of barrels abandoned just above the high water mark. 'These are brandy kegs,'

Hugh told Tom knowingly. They are called half-ankers and each holds four gallons. See how they are flat on each side? The barrel makers do that deliberately so that the tub-men can carry two of them one on their chest and the other on their back.

Tom had been counting the barrels. 'Ninety-six.'

'That's 384 gallons of brandy!' Hugh worked out. At one pound a keg someone has invested nearly £100 in this trip and will make a hefty profit unless we stop them.' Hugh was anxious that they had already been away from the castle too long. I'll go back and tell Captain Hendrick to call out his men. You keep an eye on this lot, but be careful Tom. They could be dangerous.'

Tom did not need reminding. It was less than six weeks since his gentle, loving father had been brutally murdered by men just like these. 'Don't worry. I'll keep well hidden. I want to see where they take the stuff.' As Hugh hurried back towards Portland, Tom hid himself in the sea-grass near the water's edge of the Fleet Lagoon.

It seemed only a few minutes before he heard a splashing as a body of men waded across the water. He counted between 15 and 20. *Not enough to carry the contraband inland*, he reckoned. Some of the men he could see were armed with clubs. These must be the infamous batmen, thugs whose job it was to protect the convoy of tubmen. He had already been told that as the law stood if a batman used his club on a customs officer he was unlikely to be punished by more than a few weeks in Dorchester gaol. To shoot an officer however was punishable by hanging. He couldn't see any guns.

'Isaac. Look what I've found.' Tom had failed to hear the man approach over the grass. He was hauled to his feet with his arms gripped tightly behind his back and dragged over the shingle. 'This is the new gobbler as lives in Chesilton. He's so wet behind the ears this is his first day as a bluebottle.' Tom was unceremoniously dumped on the pebbles in a circle of wet leather boots.

The last words he heard was a different voice asking 'What do we do with 'im?'

***

Tom woke to the sound of singing. He tried to sit up and immediately regretted it. His mouth was parched and his head thumped as if it was regularly being beaten by a blacksmith's hammer. He opened his eyes. Even that was an effort and he hastily closed them again. The last he remembered was being manhandled on Chesil Beach. He had sensed rather than seen the blow coming. After that he could recall nothing. A girl was still singing. She had a gentle and soothing voice and Tom hoped her singing would help him go back to sleep. The bed was so comfortable and the sheets so soft he had no ambition to do anything else but sleep, so he did.

Tom was dragged once more out of sleep by the sound of someone groaning. A cool damp cloth was pressed onto his forehead. When this was taken away his deepest wish was to feel its coolness again. He realised that it was he who was making the groaning sound. Somehow it made him feel a little better so he groaned again. The cool cloth returned.

'Mother. I think the boy's waking.'

43

A soft Dorset voice. That must be the girl who was singing, thought Tom. He opened his eyes. This time the effort was not so bad. 'Can I have some water?' he croaked. The cool cloth was removed and the girl left the room. Once more he closed his eyes and drifted back to sleep.

The third time Tom woke it was to hear the curtains being drawn and to feel the sun streaming through the window warming the room. 'Good evening, boy. How are you today?' It was a large cheerful woman who spoke. She was dressed in a simple jacket with a dark skirt half covered by a plain green apron. Her unruly hair was mostly hidden under a white linen mobcap.

'Can I have some water please?' Tom was pleased that his voice no longer sounded like a dying frog. The woman picked up a glass from the bedside table and helping him to sit upright held it to his lips. Her actions were slow and deliberate, but Tom felt a feeling of warmth and kindness from her. He swallowed a couple of mouthfuls and sank back on to the pillow. 'Thank you.' He looked round the room. 'Who are you?'

'My name is Joby de Bretton. I know that sounds French, but I am as English as you, and before you ask, you are in my home, number 2 Butter Street in the village of Fleet.'

Tom remembered the girl. 'Who was that singing?' he asked.

'That'll be my daughter Perle. She has been looking after you for the last three days. You had a nasty crack on the head and then, probably because you were soaked to the skin and frozen when you

44

arrived here, you developed a fever. We were quite worried about you for a while.'

'How did I get wet?' Tom asked.

'Jacques will explain everything to you when he gets back. Now you get some more rest. You will have some food at tea time.'

As Joby went to the door Tom asked her, 'Can I see Perle, to thank her I mean?'

'If she is free, Perle will bring your tea up.'

Tom was hungry. He hoped teatime was not too far off. Who was this Jacques who would explain everything. He lay back against the pillow and studied the tiny cottage room he had been put into. The ceiling sloped down to low walls and Tom assumed he was in some sort of attic space. One cupboard and the bed he was lying on were the only furniture. Through the tiny, floor level window he could see a grassy field and a single tree. If he had been ill for three days he wondered why Hugh and the others hadn't come searching for him. The sheets on the bed were old but clean and the bed was a hundred times more comfortable than his pile of straw in Brandy Lane. For perhaps the first time since his father had been murdered, Tom felt relaxed and at peace. Even the thumping in his head was now bearable.

It wasn't Perle carrying the tray, but a tall, serious boy, dark skinned with his hair tied at the back in a ponytail. Tom guessed he was a couple of years older than the boy. 'Hullo, I'm Jacques, but you'd better call me Jacko. Everyone does. Ma asked me to bring up your tea.'

Tom looked at the bowl of porridge and realised he was starving. Jacko helped him sit up in the bed and without further conversation Tom started to eat. Jacko seemed content to sit silently on the end of the bed studying Tom.

'Want some more?'

Tom nodded and Jacko took his bowl and returned in a few moments with it refilled. With his hunger now largely satisfied Tom ate more slowly and began to think of all the questions to which he had, as yet, no answers. 'How did I get here Jacko?'

The boy thought for a moment as if choosing his words with care then, 'I brought you.'

'Where did you find me?'

'You were lying on the shingle bank, unconscious.' Jacko answered.

'Why was I wet?'

'I had to drag you through the Fleet water to get you home.'

Getting answers out of Jacko was like pulling teeth...slow and painful. Tom realised that there was a great deal Jacko did not want to tell him. Hugh had told him the village of Fleet had a reputation for smuggling and to have a Riding Officer (even one with only one day's experience) in his house must be awkward. Tom was intelligent enough to realise he would have to get Jacques to be a little more relaxed if he wanted to get any sort of story from him. 'Jacko, you know I am with the Customs Service. I must have been wearing my uniform when you carried me here. It seems likely that, by bringing me to your home, you have saved my life. I promise I will not betray you or your companions and friends. I

46

will not report anything I learn in this house. You must believe me.' Tom could see that Jacko was not yet convinced. 'Do you have a bible?'

Jacko went to the door and whispered to someone who must have been listening outside. There was another uncomfortable silence until a girl carrying a large family bible cautiously entered and limped over to the bed.

'This is my sister Perle. She's the one who has been looking after you for the last few days.'

Perle stood next to the bed with her eyes looking down shyly. She held out the bible to Tom. He wanted to thank her but guessed he would have to gain Jacko's confidence first before he was allowed to talk to her. He took the bible from her and laying it on the sheet, placed his right hand on the gold cross, inlaid in the red leather cover. 'I promise before God that whatever I hear in this house that might harm the de Bretton family or their companions and friends will remain a confidence between them and me until the day of my death. So help me God.'

Jacko took the bible from him and smiled for the first time.

Chapter 5
Friendly Faces

'Our father was French.' Jacques de Bretton sat on the end of Tom's bed munching on a lump of cheese. 'He was called Guy and was a free trader...what you would call a smuggler. It's his nightshirt you're wearing. He first came over to England during the time of peace in Napoleon's wars and married mother. I don't think he ever felt any loyalty to either the English or French governments, as he carried on trading even when war started again. Then on one voyage when he tried to run the English blockade of Le Havre, his boat *L'Hirondelle – The Swallow* in English, was sunk. Mother never heard what happened to him, but he probably drowned. Perle was only three when that happened and I was four.'

In the two days since Tom had regained consciousness Perle and Jacko had been regular visitors to his room. At first Perle had been reluctant to speak to him unless her brother was present but this day she had stayed behind after bringing his lunch and talked to him, shyly at first and then with increasing confidence. Tom thought she was very pretty and not unlike his sister Amanda in character, though a year younger. Perle had the same colouring and button brown eyes as Jacques, but lacked her brother's confidence and swagger. Tom had little experience with girls other than his two sisters. There was one occasion when a friend of Amanda called Cordelia had tried to kiss him, but the clumsy effort had embarrassed both of them. Tom was happier reading about love in his Latin texts than trying the real thing. By treating Perle as he would have treated Amanda or Beth, she had started to lose her shyness. Tom noticed she had a limp as if her left leg was shorter than the right, but she tried to disguise this by moving slowly around the room and sitting down whenever she could. He guessed she already found excuses to come and sit on his bed for a chat.

In one of their conversations she had told him that this room was usually hers. 'I'm sleeping with mother while you're here. I do that whenever we have visitors.'

Tom told her about his mother's death and the tragic murder of his father in Sixpenny Handley. She wanted to know everything about Amanda and Beth and Tom told her stories of their childhood and his own thwarted ambitions to go to university. He decided it would be sensible not to tell her about the Coast Guard Service. His limited experience so far was something he preferred to put out of his mind.

The morning after Tom had made his oath on the bible Jacko had told him how he had found him on the beach. 'On the night of the landing I had been employed as a look out for the free traders. I saw one of the batmen strike you hard on the back of the head and dump you on the pebbles. The tubmen then carried off the brandy and the lander, I'll not tell you his name, ordered all of us to leave you where you were. I didn't dare do anything at that time, but when the landing party had all gone, Mother suggested I go back to check on you. You were still unconscious but looked in a bad way, so I decided to carry you back home over the lagoon. I couldn't just leave you there to die.' Next day, Joby de Bretton had sent Jacko with a message to Captain Bouscarle in Weymouth telling him where Tom could be found. 'A weasily little man called Arthur rode out to check on you. He said he would send a letter to the castle on Portland and he asked us to look after you until you had recovered. He gave mother two shillings to pay for your food.' *That'll come out of my next month's salary*, thought Tom.

On one visit to Tom's room Perle chatted about her mother's work as a cook in the Lugger Inn in Chickerell. 'I go and help her sometimes when there's a lot of people and will probably work full time there next year if I don't get a job in the big house at Waddon. Ma wants Jacko to take an apprenticeship as a carpenter, though he's probably already too old for that. She's worried that he will want to join the smugglers and will end up dead like our father. Jacko says he wants to be a sailor and own his own ship.'

On another visit, Perle told him how on moonless nights when she was warm in bed she would hear 'the Gentlemen of the Night' tramping past the cottage window. 'I expect I know many of them as most of the folks around here are involved in *The Trade*,' she told Tom. 'Mother won't let me see who they are, though I'm sure she knows. Someone important, who knew our father, gives her money regularly, but I don't know who that is either.'

By the fourth day of his recovery Tom felt stronger and asked if he could go for a short walk. Jacko offered to come with him and lent him some old clothes. 'People around here don't trust men in your uniform,' he explained. 'Ma has kept quiet about your staying here in case the lander gets to hear of it. I don't want to explain to him how I rescued you from the beach, but I expect he will find out if he doesn't know already.'

The two young men walked down the street to the little church, passing the pub at the end of Butter Street know locally as the *Why Not?* 'Best not to go in there,' Jacko warned him. 'They don't like customs men.'

Tom told him of his experiences on Portland and in particular at The Cove House Inn.

'You've got to understand,' Jacko tried hard to explain, 'everyone around here is involved in *The Trade* somewhere. Even mother, who strongly disapproves of it, would be forced to admit that her wage at The Lugger is largely paid for by selling smuggled brandy.' He sat down on one gravestone and Tom sat opposite him on another.

'Smuggling is against the law,' Tom said firmly. 'If we don't obey the law the country will end up in chaos like the French.' Even to himself Tom sounded insufferably stuffy, however he pressed on. 'My father used to say that after God's law there was nothing more sacred than the Common Law of England. If he hadn't been killed I would have gone to Oxford to read law. The law of the land must be obeyed. You admit that even your mother is against smuggling. It doesn't make it any more right calling it *The Trade*. It's still smuggling.'

'Mother's against *The Trade* because she's frightened what might happen to me,' Jacko said stubbornly. He recognised that he would probably be out-gunned by Tom in an argument, but he knew he had a valid point of view, which he was determined to put across. 'What if it's bad law? Hasn't everyone a right even a duty to disobey bad law? The free traders buy goods in France. They don't steal them. Then they sell them on in England. That sounds like honest trading to me. A few years ago the government passed a law to keep the price of corn high enough so that the landowners could make a comfortable profit. No one seemed to worry that poor folk would no longer be able to afford to buy bread. Every year labourers' wages are falling and if it wasn't for the little bit of cash folk around here make from what you call smuggling, we would all starve.' Jacko was speaking with passion now. These were arguments he had heard many times from the folk in the bar of The Lugger Inn. 'The men who help in *The Trade* are not thieves. They are quarrymen, tin-plate workers, flax-dressers, butchers and farm labourers, all honest workingmen. A week's wage for a labourer in Dorset is seven or eight shillings. That is not enough for a man to feed his family. For a night's work helping those you call smugglers, a tubman might earn between five and seven shillings. That is the difference between food for his children and starvation.'

There was a tense silence as the two young men sat on their respective gravestones glaring at each other. 'That's what I think anyhow,' Jacko said eventually holding Tom's look, 'and there's a lot around here as agrees with me. And they are not all poor folk either. Now I must go to collect something for Ma from Weymouth,' he said sullenly.

Before Tom could think how to answer, Jacko had disappeared down the road. It had unsettled Tom to hear such a passionate argument in favour of smuggling though deep down he still believed what his father had said about the law. He walked slowly and thoughtfully across the churchyard and up Butter Street. *How awkward has it been for Joby, Jacko and Perle to have a customs man living in their house*, he wondered. *I should have thought of that earlier. They've never once made things difficult for me or even hinted at it. Now I've recovered, I suppose it's time I went back to Portland.* He didn't relish the idea of working for Saul Overton but in his financial situation he had little choice. *A bit like the smugglers*, he though uncomfortably.

Perle was alone in the kitchen making bread. 'Where is your mother?' Tom asked.

'She has been called up to The Lugger. There's a stage-coach load from Exeter spending the night and Isaac has asked her to work late.'

'Who is Isaac?' Tom asked. The name seemed familiar, but he could not immediately place it.

'Isaac is the landlord at The Lugger,' Perle answered. 'He's always been very good to us.'

Tom had a memory flash of someone holding his arms behind his back and saying '*Isaac, look what I've found,*' just before he lost consciousness. He looked at Perle, was about to speak and quickly decided not to say anything more. He slumped into the oak rocking chair, which dominated the corner of the kitchen.

'What's the matter Tom?' Perle asked tentatively. 'You look sort of sad.'

'I am sad. It's time I went back to work and I don't want to leave here. Also I've just had a row with Jacko, and I didn't want that either.'

Perle turned abruptly away to fiddle with the kettle on the stove before he could see the look of panic on her face. 'Do you want a cup of tea?' she asked in a tiny voice. 'The water's just boiled.'

'Yes please.' Tom wondered briefly why he found dealing with Perle so simple. *Perhaps,* he thought, *it's because I can treat her just like Amanda or Beth.* He wanted to ask her what was wrong with her leg, but felt uneasily that this question might upset her. Perhaps when he knew her better he would ask.

There was nothing sisterly about Perle's feelings for Tom. She blushed as she remembered that first night helping her mother strip off his wet clothes. There were boys in Chickerell who said they fancied her but she just found them tiresome. She was excited at the thought of this handsome young man sleeping in her bed even if it meant she had to be in with her mother. She ducked her head in embarrassment. 'Must you go?' Perle tried to stop her voice squeaking, but she was finding it difficult to breath. 'Mother says it's all right if you stay for a bit more and don't worry about Jacko. He will have forgotten all about whatever it was by tomorrow.'

'I'm sorry but I must.' He was touched by the thought that Joby and Perle wanted him to stay. 'It's my duty to start work as soon as I can.' *When I talk about my work, why do I sound so stuck up?* He wondered.

'I'll iron your uniform tonight.' The constriction in Perle's chest felt a little easier. 'It was terribly crumpled after being soaked.' She knew her mother had already carefully ironed it on Tom's first day at the cottage, but it would do no harm for her to give it a second ironing. She suddenly had a flash of inspiration. 'The Saturday after next is the start of Portesham Fayre's week. Jacko and I always go. If you would like to come with us you could be here at nine o'clock that morning.' It seemed like minutes as she waited for his answer.

'What a grand idea. If I can get time off I'll definitely come.'

Perle smiled at the kettle.

Chapter 6
Rough Justice

Tom stood in Overton's office counting the squares on the carpet. Captain Bouscarle had warned him that Saul Overton was not very pleased, but he had not expected this public humiliation. *One green, three red, one green three red...* 'Well, Vermin, what have you got to say for yourself?'

Tom had stopped listening to Overton's tirade some minutes go. He tried to think of a suitably neutral response. 'Nothing to say Sir.' He continued to stare at the carpet but let his mind wander again. Joby de Bretton had made it clear that she was sorry to see him go. He had told Jacko next morning that he felt it was time he went back to work and far from bearing a grudge over their argument Jacko had hoped that the two of them would keep in touch.

Captain Bouscarle had seemed pleased that he had recovered and had warned him that Lieutenant Overton seemed irritated by his absence. Arthur, as expected, had advised him that any money given to Mrs de Bretton would be taken out of his wages.

Tom was worried about Gussie so before reporting back to Portland Castle, he called in at the cottage in Brandy Row. The stable was empty but he found Sam Ditchburn with the horse on the grass of Verne Common. 'I heard you were having a spot of bother,' the old man smiled at him, 'and so I's been looking after this old chap till you got back.'

Tom was grateful, but also intrigued. 'How did you know I was unwell?'

'All the folks hereabouts knew. I heard someone talking in The Cove House Inn.' Sam waved his hand to demonstrate vague rumours flying through the air. Tom, realising he was unlikely to get any more information from Sam, didn't press him. He was absurdly touched by this show of genuine kindness from a Portlander. 'I don't think that lootenant of yours is very pleased with you.' Sam appeared to hesitate as to how much he should say. 'I believe your little trip cost him a good-sized *bunce*. Ten *georges* is what I heard.' Sam paused to scratch his beard. 'Not a very nice man your lootenant.'

Tom had plenty to think about as he and Gussie plodded the short distance to Portland castle. Possibly Overton would be upset that he had been injured on an unauthorised expedition. He might even have been concerned about his injury. He couldn't understand how his initiative might have cost him ten sovereigns. Perhaps Hugh would be able to shed some light on that. But when he arrived at the Castle he couldn't find Hugh and when he reported to Overton he was immediately dragged into the office where Matthew and another Riding Officer, who Tom assumed was Henry, had obviously been ordered to witness Tom's humiliation.

As Overton wound up his rant Tom dragged his attention back to what the lieutenant was saying. 'You will never again go on little unauthorised missions, do you understand? Untrained as you are, you know nothing about what we do here. What Riding Officer Dawkins called using his initiative set back our work by weeks.'

'Where is Hugh?' Tom asked.

'Riding Officer Dawkins has left the island.' Tom could see out of the corner of his eye that Matthew was looking uncomfortable. 'I believe his father is unwell and he has gone home. He will not be returning to this station.'

'Am I to move into his quarters?'

'What makes you think we want a cockroach like you living with us here. Go back to your hovel and learn to do what you are told.'

This was grossly unfair to Tom. He had not disobeyed orders. He hadn't been given any orders. He opened his mouth to speak but Overton hadn't finished yet.

'Now Dawkins has gone, you can do my laundry, Vermin.' He turned to leave the room but Tom had had enough.

'No Sir.'

'What did you say?' Overton strode over to where Tom was standing. He tried to stand tall, but the man's face, working in fury, was genuinely frightening.

'I said no Sir; I will not do your laundry. I believe it is not part of my duties to wash an officer's clothes.'

'Not part of your duties.' Tom felt the specks of spittle spatter his face. 'Your duty is to do exactly what I tell you, no more no less.' Tom did not see the blow coming, but Overton put all his considerable weight and strength into a swinging punch to Tom's stomach. He fell to the floor shocked and winded. As he lay there gasping for air, Overton strode from the room.

At first no one else in the room moved. Tom was incapable of doing anything and the other two appeared frozen by shock. In the distance a door slammed and the sound allowed Henry to come over to the winded boy. 'You shouldn't have said that,' Henry whispered. 'We've all done our turn with washing his clothes. If you do what he says, it's just about bearable here. If he takes against you... well see what happened to Dawkins.'

Tom slowly forced air back into his lungs. He was grey with pain and his forehead felt clammy with sweat. With Henry's help he staggered to his feet and was half dragged and half carried over to one of the benches. Matthew, who had not said a word since Tom had entered the wardroom, unfroze himself and shuffled out. 'What did happen to Hugh?' Tom was eventually able to ask.

'The evening the two of you went to Chesil, Overton had already returned from his trip on *Samphire* before Dawkins was able to get back here. When Dawkins told him what the two of you had seen Overton went berserk and beat him up horribly. When Matthew came back from his patrol he cleaned him up as best he could. Next day Dawkins was sent from the island. I don't know what story Overton told, but we have heard nothing since. Overton pretended to Matthew and me that everything that happened that night had been part of one big plan, and we were sworn to silence.'

'Could you get me a drink of water,' Tom said. 'I don't think I can move yet.'
When Henry returned with a mug of water Tom asked him to go on with the story.

'I think next evening Overton was sent a message from Weymouth probably from Arthur saying that you had been found injured, and wouldn't be coming back to work for a bit. From his attitude I honestly think he was a bit disappointed that you hadn't just quietly disappeared. Anyhow he has been in a foul mood ever since.' He paused and shook his head. 'You shouldn't have said that about the washing.'

'Why does he hate me so much?'

'He hates everyone. All of us have learned in time that it's best to do what he says without question. Don't be proud. Do his washing.'

Tom suddenly remembered something that Sam Ditchburn had said. 'One of the fishermen in Chesilton told me Overton had lost a good-sized *bunce*. What did be mean by that?'

Henry was not to be drawn. He clammed up and walked to the other side of the wardroom saying nothing. Eventually he turned back to Tom. 'Best not to ask questions like that.'

'What do I do now Henry? I don't want to take another beating like that.'

Henry thought for a moment. 'If I was in your position I would agree to do his laundry or that will become a major challenge to him. Come over to the castle early every day for work, but try keeping out of Overton's way. Because you are not living here you might be able to avoid him most of the time and you should learn his routines as quickly as possible. He will certainly give you the worst watches to keep until he has another victim to pick on.'

Tom tried hard to follow most of Henry's advice, but he was not prepared to wash Overton's clothes.

At the end of the week Matthew told him on Overton's instruction that his salary hadn't come through. Matthew lent him five shillings so that at least he wouldn't starve. As expected he had to work the longest hours. Overton explained that with Hugh absent all of them would have to share his duties, but it was noticeable that it was Tom who was given most of the extra work. For the next seven day he did little but work and sleep becoming more and more exhausted.

Towards the end of the week he was dragging himself back to his barren little cottage when Sam Ditchburn met him in Brandy Row. 'Come into The Cove for a glass of grog, Son. You look as if you need it.'

Tom was absurdly grateful for the touch of kindness this showed. He sat in the taproom of The Cove House Inn and unburdened himself to Sam who proved to be a good listener. 'I warned you Overton was not a very kindly fellow. He is liked neither by the King's men nor the Free Traders. He is a bully and no one trusts him.'

Tom finished his beer and stood up embarrassed. 'I'm sorry I can't buy my round Sam. The Lieutenant has managed to lose my pay. When it is eventually found I would like to return your kindness.'

'Don't worry yourself lad. There'll be plenty of time for that later. Watch out for the weather tomorrow. The wind has swung round and the glass is falling. We are in for a storm and my guess is that it will be a good 'un.'

'At least that means that French luggers are unlikely to anchor in Lyme Bay.' Tom saw he had made the old man smile.

Chapter 7
Wreck of the Arethusa

The wind beat against the windows of The Cove House Inn, rattling the glass in the leaded frames. Every time the door opened to let in another weather-soaked customer a rush of cold air and rain accompanied him. Round the fire in the taproom a group of young men sat morosely hugging their beer pots complaining about their inability to fish. August should have been a key month for mackerel, but the summer gale showed no sign of blowing itself out. Tom was sitting with Sam Ditchburn in the same corner they had occupied the day before. He had chosen to be in civilian clothes as Sam had warned him that the sight of the revenue officer's blue uniform made the customers of Cove House uneasy. Although Sam was the only inhabitant of Chesilton who regularly spoke to him, others now greeted him and a few knew his name. The storm had built up throughout the day and Overton, knowing that any illicit activities would be impossible, had sent Tom and Matthew off early

Sam was demonstrating to Tom how the quarrymen of Portland handled such massive blocks of stone and in particular how they loaded the barges without accidents, when once again the door crashed open and a young fisherman, who Tom vaguely recognised, came over to the group by the fire. He was obviously excited and began to give them an animated account of something he had seen. 'Wait here lad,' Sam said to him and ambled over to listen to what the young man had to say. After a couple of questions he returned to the table where Tom still sat. 'Mikey's come from near the lookout rock. He says that there's a brig just rounded the Bill and entered the Bay. She must have come inside The Shambles sand bar. 'Tis likely she got caught up in The Race.'

'What's The Race?' Tom asked.

Sam gripped his pint pot and gazed towards the storm-thrashed window. 'The Race off Portland Bill is one of the most violent stretches of water in all the northern seas,' he answered. 'If the tides are running strong the race is a savage waste of white sea, which seethes and bubbles like a boiling pot and screams and yells most terrifically. It is a wicked place for the unwary and no sailor who knows these waters, when sailing from the East, would dare encounter it when there's a sou'westerly gale blowing. If Daniel is right and it is a brig which has rounded The Bill, there are likely to be bodies on the beach by morning.'

The group of young men had pulled on jackets and left the inn, but Sam sat puffing on his pipe. 'There is no need for hurry. Probably the captain himself is not yet aware of the danger he's in. See, the foremast of the brig is square rigged. This means she cannot sail closer than three points to the wind. In a normal sea with the wind from the sou'west this would allow the captain to set a course from the Bill directly across to Torquay or at least the mouth of the Exe. As he crosses the Bay he can put onto the starboard tack and gain as much sea room as he needs. But this is neither a normal sea nor tide. With this gale, unless the wind changes to blow from the south, the further he enters Lyme Bay the more the tides and wind are going to push his ship towards the land. He probably feels he is safer in the bay than turning south to risk The Shambles and The Race again but sadly the tide won't give him the searoom he needs to weather The Bill a second time. Every tack he makes he will be pushed closer to our bay here. There's a good reason this be called Dead Man's Cove. Very shortly the captain will realise that his only choice is whether he is going to beach on Chesil or Portland.' Tom had a hundred questions to ask but Sam had knocked out his pipe and started to put on his jacket. 'Come outside. If the brig is in sight, I can explain it better. It still wants three hours till it's dark. There's plenty of folk here will try to make sure this doesn't become a tragedy, but if she does end up in the cove there will be pickings for all of us in the morning.'

Outside, despite the howling wind and lashing rain, a small crowd had already collected in front of the inn. The roar of the pounding surf on the pebbles was deafening and in the distance through the storm Tom could make out the shadowy shape of a ship struggling through the waves getting ever closer to Chesil Beach. A figure in boots and a waterproof stomped over next to Sam. 'Evening, Sam. Captain's just taken in her topsails and topgallants. Reckon he's going to try to work her with the spanker and the foresails. He must be hoping this will allow him to sail close enough to clear this Bill.'

As he spoke Tom could see the ship go about and push her bows through the wind. It seemed to him a slow and laboured business. The tide, pushing eastwards, grabbed at the bows to force them away from the course the captain wished to steer.

Gradually the brig picked up steerageway on the new tack and started to crawl back towards the watchers. 'She'll not make it on that tack,' Sam muttered. 'Captain's only hope is to try again on the port tack without his square rig.' As he spoke the brig again tacked but the manoeuvre was sluggish as once more the tide dragged her back towards Portland. When at last she started to move forward, it was obvious even to Tom that she was even closer to the waiting arms of Dead Man's Cove. 'Captain will likely take off all the canvas and try to anchor,' Sam told him. 'But unless you know where is the one small patch of good holding ground, no anchor will grab.'

Almost immediately the sails began to shiver and flap and the brig turned directly towards the inn. She rushed towards them pushed by the wind and tide and 200 yards off shore the Captain tried to bring her round into the wind dropping his bow anchor at the same time. As she presented her stern to the shore someone with a spyglass shouted out 'She's the *Arethusa*, out from Bremen.' From his classics lessons Tom briefly remembered that Arethusa was one of the nymphs pursued by the water god Alphaeus. Never before had such knowledge seemed quite so useless. For a moment, as the *Arethusa* shuddered to a halt, it appeared against all odds that the captain had succeeded. Then, with a dreadful inevitability, the ship began to drag stern first towards the beach.

Sam had earlier told Tom that a brig could be crewed by 12 to 16 men. Through the telescope he could see a small group of about that number huddled round the main mast waving frantically to those on shore. The doomed ship slid closer and closer to the surf and eventually crunched on the pebbles a mere 30 yards from dry land. Wave after wave pounded into her and occasionally washed right over the bows. Tom tore his eyes from the scene. 'Can't we do something to help those men?' he begged Sam.

'It's too rough to launch the lerret. Some of the young men asked if they could row out with a line, but I have told them it's not possible. We would only make the tragedy worse.' As he spoke Tom saw that one of the fishermen was trying to hurl a line to the stricken vessel, but it was carried by the wind and fell well short. 'I expect they will try sending Bowser out,' he said pointing up the beach. Bowser one of the celebrated Portland sea dogs with webbed feet already had a thin cord attached to his collar. His master pointed towards the stricken vessel and the dog launched himself into the waves only to be dashed back onto the beach. He tried a second time angling his leap so that he didn't meet the wave head on, but the result was the same. 'The crew could send a line to us by floating a barrel down the wind,' Sam said, 'but by this stage they are usually too panicked to think straight. They will start jumping soon. Our lads will try to grab them, but the undertow usually wins.'

Tom, anxious to do anything to help hurried down to the shore line and asked to join the column of young men preparing to reach into the surf. He wrapped his belt round the rope to get a better grip and dug his heels into the pebbles. Each successive wave pounded the *Arethusa* more and she began to break up piece by piece under the hammering. To the despairing crew safety must have seemed tantalisingly close. The human chain of Chesilton men, each one linked to another by rope, stretched from the pebble bank into the breaking waves. As each doomed sailor leaped for the shore his body was dashed by the breakers and dragged out to sea by the undertow. Each time the head of the column of men, like some giant serpent stretching towards its prey, reached out unavailingly into the savage water. Every few minutes the man at the head of the line would stagger ashore and be replaced by the next man.

Tom found himself getting nearer and nearer to the waves. When it was his turn to head the line the man next behind him passed the rope end round his waist. Tom turned to make sure it was held secure and the young man, a fisherman who he didn't know, grinned at him in the gathering gloom. One of the fast diminishing cluster on the ship leaped for the shore and Tom struggled out into the sea to try to grab at him, at the moment the next wave smashed down. As the undertow seized him he felt the rope round his waist tighten, squeezing the air out of his lungs. He flailed around with his arms despairingly hoping to find anything to grab on to. He staggered back to his feet and the next wave pounded in. After two more drubbings Tom felt a tap on his shoulder and relieved, staggered back out of the water where willing hands helped him up the beach. Not many minutes later, with nothing now moving on the foredeck of the *Arethusa,* the young men reckoned they could do no more and reluctantly the line broke up as they pulled back to higher ground.

Darkness fell and the crowd watched the death throes of a once fine ship. Now was not the time for scavenging. Gradually the crowd left the beach with the wind and waves still pounding and returned to the safety of their houses.

By next morning the gale had blown itself out. Tom went straight to the beach early but was by no means the first to arrive. He counted eight bodies carefully laid out above the high water mark. 'There will be more along the coast to the south,' one of the fishermen said to him. Tom reckoned this was the first comment anyone from Chesilton other than Sam had passed to him. He tried to start a conversation but the man walked away down the beach in silence. The pebble bank was covered with the debris of planks and cordage and a sad group of scavengers sifted through it. The sight depressed him so he collected an armful of driftwood for his fire and returned to his cottage. Though Lieutenant Overton had reluctantly agreed that there would be no work over the weekend, Tom thought it advisable that he should report the wreck of the *Arethusa* and the drowning of the crew to Portland Castle. Lieutenant Overton received the news with apparent indifference. Having done his duty Tom set off for the village of Fleet to see Perle and Jacko, a meeting he had been looking forward to all week.

Chapter 8
Portesham Fayre

Perle had very nearly given up waiting for Tom. She had been ready to go, in her best smocking pinafore, for at least two hours. Jacko, impatient to be with his friends, had already set off for Portesham 90 minutes earlier. Joby was irritated by her daughter's mooning around and had tried to get her to leave with Jacko. When this failed, she had set her to work trying to keep the girl occupied. At last Perle, keeping watch out of her bedroom window spotted Gussie and Tom coming over the hill along the coast road. She rushed downstairs and busily occupied herself with sweeping, feigning indifference when there was at last a knock on the door. Joby, who was in no way fooled by her daughter's distraction, let Tom in.

'I'm so sorry I am late.' Tom explained the circumstances of his delay.

Joby thought he looked tired and unwell. She had expected that in the ten days since he had left her house he would have regained his strength. 'Don't worry about it Tom. Perle has finished her chores and I am sure she's just about ready to leave. Your pony will be safe here and I will make sure he is fed and watered. Jacques is not here. He left for Portesham quite a while ago. He said he would meet you there.' Perle, sensitive enough to know that her mother had tried hard to make things easy for her, kissed her on the cheek. Joby discreetly pressed three shillings into the girl's hand. 'Go on and enjoy yourself child.'

It looked as if all 150 of the inhabitants of Portesham had collected on the glebe field and along the main street for the opening of the summer fair. Tom had been telling Perle about Lieutenant Overton's violent attack on him and the campaign of hate that followed. Perle had been able to offer very little advice or comfort and the conversation had left both of them feeling miserable. As they crossed the road into the fair ground they were met by a blast of sound and colour. This was the first village fete Tom had been to. There seemed to be a great deal of laughter, singing and general noise compared to the gloomy silences of Portland Castle or even the dark suspicion with which he was met in Chesilton. 'Come and have something to drink.' Perle dragged him over to a table where an old man was selling elderflower cordial.

'I know it's silly, but I don't have any money.' Tom was acutely aware of his ridiculous position in coming to a summer fair penniless.

'Good Morning Perle.' Tom swung round to see a smiling, middle-aged lady accompanied by three teenage girls, advancing towards them. 'Surely this isn't your brother Jacques?'

'That's not Jacko, Mama,' the eldest of the three girls interrupted. 'Is he here Perle?'

'Good morning Lady Hardy.' Perle bobbed a curtsey. 'This is a friend of mine Tom Verney. He's an officer in the Coast Guard. Jacko's here somewhere Louisa, though we haven't found him yet.'

71

'Can I go round the fair with Perle Mama?' The middle of the three girls begged her mother. 'Please Mama.'

A moment of concern crossed Lady Hardy's face. 'Are you sure you will be all right Emily?'

It was obvious that the girl was desperate to accompany Tom and Perle. Tom remembered the many occasions he had chaperoned his sisters and thought there was no harm in making an offer. 'I will make sure she is safe Ma'am.' When he spoke for the first time his cultured accent reassured the anxious mother. 'What time would you like her to be home?'

'Thank you.' She nodded graciously. 'Why don't you all come for some tea around four? The fair will be finishing by then, and bring your scamp of a brother Perle if you can find him. I'm sure Louisa would like that.' Louisa denied it hotly, but her blush suggested that her mother's little dart had been accurately thrown. 'Come along Charlotte,' she said to the littlest girl who was nervously holding her mother's hand. 'I promised to show you the monkey man.' With that she swept away.

Perle was not overjoyed at the thought of Emily joining her and Tom. She had hoped to have him all to herself, but as it turned out Emily's presence did nothing but good. Her infectious high spirits soon lifted the gloom from both of them and the two girls chattered away together. Tom following behind realised he was enjoying himself just being in their company. There wasn't anything in the fair that was dramatically exciting. Perle seemed to know most of the young people present, but did not feel it necessary to introduce Tom all the time. At one stall she bought a honeycomb for her mother, and at another three toffee apples. The three of them munched their way round to the fire-eater and the monkey man and the stilt walkers. Only the monkey proved to be a disappointment. It was obviously tired of performing and sat immovable on its stick. Eventually the best it could do was to bare its teeth at them.

They were inspecting the vegetables on display on the lawn in front of the King's Arms when Emily said, 'There's Jacko.' He was sitting with a group of local lads all of who looked as if they had already drunk a reasonable amount of ale. He staggered to his feet grinning, obviously delighted to see Tom again.

'Hi Tom. Been in any more scraps recently?' He noticed Emily standing next to his sister. 'Hullo Em. Come over and meet my friends Tom. You'll like them.'

The idea of sitting down and having a pint of ale with a group of boys his own age appealed to Tom, but once again his sense of duty held him back. 'I promised Emily's mother I would look after her Jacko. I'll see you later.'

'Lady Hardy kindly invited you to tea at four o'clock,' Perle told him sternly. 'But you had better not show up if you drink any more. Em's father is at home.'

This last comment, elliptical to Tom, seemed to sober Jacko. 'Say thank you to your ma Em, but I don't think I will be able to make it.'

As the hands on the Reverend Verney's pocket watch reached 4.00 pm Tom and Perle delivered Emily safely back to the front door of Portesham House. The imposing building made of grey Portland stone stood at the edge of the village. Perle urged Tom not to be scared. She explained that when she was small her mother had worked as the housekeeper for Lady Hardy and she had grown up in the house and made friends with all three girls, 'but Emily has always been my special friend.' Tom was used to large imposing vicarages and did not feel overawed by the occasion.

'Come in dears.' Lady Hardy welcomed the two of them into an impressive drawing room. Everything in that beautifully proportioned room spoke of style and money. Tom wished he had been a little more smartly turned out. He would have felt more comfortable in his uniform, but none of the Hardy family seemed to be standing on their dignity and he tried to relax. 'Charlotte, find your father and tell him that tea is to be served in the drawing room. He will be in his cabin.' she tinkled a small silver hand bell. 'It's not really a cabin,' she explained to Tom, 'but that is what my husband likes to call his study. Sit next to me and tell me about yourself Mr Verney.'

Tom began to tell the story of his father's sudden death in Sixpenny Handley and how circumstances had forced him to give up any idea of university and take up his godfather's offer of work in the Coast Guard service. 'I am quite content, but I worry for my two sisters who are much the same age as Miss Louisa and Miss Emily. I have only had one letter from them since I came to Portland…'

Tom stopped as Lady Hardy's husband entered. 'What have you girls brought home this time?' he asked cheerfully. A presence of great authority filled the room. He was not tall, and aged in his mid fifties had begun to grow quite stout. His nut-brown hair had receded leaving a large domed forehead. 'Hullo, Perle. I haven't seen you for quite a long time,' he smiled at her and turned to Tom. 'Who is this young man?'

'This is Mr Verney dear. He was just telling us about the tragic death of his father, the vicar of Sixpenny Handley. Mr Verney this is my husband, Commodore Hardy.'

'Yes, nasty business. I remember reading about it.' He shook Tom's hand. 'What do you do Mr Verney?'

Tom stood with his mouth open unable to speak. This was the man who had captained *Victory* at Trafalgar and cradled the dying Nelson. How stupid of him not to have realised who Lady Hardy's husband was. He could think of nothing to say.

'It's all right Tom.' Emily came up to him and squeezed his arm. 'Father often has that effect on people. Tom's in the Coast Guard service father and has been telling us about a dreadful wreck on Portland yesterday. What was the name of the ship Tom?'

'*Arethusa*,' Tom croaked. His mind was still reeling. The man who had just shaken his hand was one of Nelson's *Band of Brothers* at the battle of the Nile and it was rumoured that once, when Thomas Hardy was still a lieutenant, Nelson had risked his own ship to save him from being captured. Tom's father had gloried in the successes of the British Navy and Tom had been brought up on stories of Nelson, Jervis, Collingwood and Hardy.

Sir Thomas Hardy, who had often seen young midshipmen struck dumb when questioned by a senior naval officer, took pity on Tom. 'Come and sit here young man. I want to know all the details. Yesterday's gale was a sou'wester. I suppose she was caught on a lee shore?'

Tom sat down on the sofa next to Sir Thomas. He tried hard to remember the sequence of events that Sam had described to him. When he mentioned the *Arethusa* weathering Portland Bill and The Shambles the Commodore quickly asked him what type of boat she had been. 'She was a two-masted brig,' Tom answered. 'It was some while before the captain realised he was in danger. With the tide running from west to east he wasn't able to gain enough sea room.' Tom was quietly proud that he was able to give a good account of the incident.

Those in the room could see that Sir Thomas was picturing the struggle as the doomed vessel tried to claw its way to safety. 'Didn't the captain attempt to sail her to safety using his fore and aft sails?

Tom remembered what he had been told. 'He loosened the square rig and tried to sail to windward with the spanker and foresail, but by then it was too late. He also tried to anchor in Deadman's Cove, but it wouldn't hold and the ship was crushed by the waves.'

Commodore Hardy was impressed by Tom's description and could picture the disaster clearly. For years taking part in the navy's blockade of France during the war against Napoleon, he had seen incautious captains allow their ships to venture too close to the shore of France. Captains who were unaware of the dangerous combination of a 10 knot tide stream and a south-westerly wind, failing to claw their way seaward, would in time be dashed on the rocks off Ushant. 'Poor devils. Were there any survivors?'

'Tom tried to save those on the ship by joining a long line of men going into the waves,' Emily butted in. Tom could see that his conversation was the centre of all attention. He sensed that it was important to all of them, well Perle and Emily certainly, that he held his own with Sir Thomas. 'They also tried sending out a poor dog to rescue them.'

Her father smiled at his daughter 'The famous Portland sea-dogs with webbed feet. I imagine the dog was safe enough wasn't it Tom?'

Tom could see that Sir Thomas was trying to reassure Emily who was obviously more concerned about the fate of Bowser than the sailors. He nodded. 'Yes he was quite safe.' He wanted to ask a question that had been bothering him ever since he had watched the men of the *Arethusa* jump into the sea the day before. He sensed that the conversation was about to move on. Neither Sir Thomas nor Lady Hardy wished to dwell any longer on the fate of drowned sailors, but he was determined not to miss this opportunity. 'All the crew were lost Sir, even though the wreck was less than 30 yards from the shore. The Portlanders tried every way they could to get a line to the ship. If they had managed it I am sure nearly all of the crew could have been saved.' He paused trying to phrase his question carefully. 'Surely someone in the navy has developed a system for getting a rope to a stricken ship that is more effective than hurling a line attached to a marlin spike?'

'That is a very good question.' Sir Thomas thought for a moment. 'We should talk of something else now, but come along to the cabin after tea. Can't stay here chatting. I have work to do.' He levered himself out of the chair and left the room, back to his cabin Tom presumed.

He felt embarrassed that the great man had snubbed him, but he looked across towards the girls and they were all relaxed and smiling. It was almost as if he had passed some sort of test.

'How is your leg dear?' Lady Hardy, well meaning but insensitive, spoke to Perle who blushed and wriggled uncomfortably on her chair. 'As a child she scalded her leg badly in my kitchen when Joby used to work here,' she explained to Tom. 'I have always felt guilty about it.'

'It's fine now thank you. Doesn't hurt a bit.' Perle sat there biting her lip, obviously desperately uncomfortable at the turn of the conversation.

Tom did not like seeing anyone so obviously ill at ease and thought quickly to change the conversation. 'Is your husband on leave at this time, Lady Hardy? It must be good to have him at home.' Perle smiled at him shyly, grateful for his intervention.

'He's quite recently back from South America.' Lady Hardy was always happy to talk about her husband's career. She chattered away about captains and ships that meant nothing to Tom. 'He asked to see you dear. If you have finished your tea, you had better not keep him waiting.'

The cabin was one of the smallest rooms in Portesham House. There was some view of the garden out of the small window but the room was small, dark and comfortable and decidedly masculine. When Tom entered Sir Thomas was already sitting beside his desk smoking a small cheroot. He invited Tom to sit down in an old leather armchair. 'M'Lady doesn't like me smoking in the house, but I can do what I like in my cabin,' he explained. 'None of the females ever comes in here.'

Tom realised that it was a privilege to be invited into this inner sanctuary. He looked round the room at walls smothered in paintings, etchings and, almost covering one wall, a tattered white ensign. 'Was that from *HMS Victory*?' Tom asked pointing at the flag.

'No m' boy. Lord Nelson had *Victory's* battle ensign covering his coffin on the sad day of his funeral. Then it was handed to Lady Nelson. This is the ensign flown by *Mutine* at the battle of the Nile. She was my first command. All I have to remember *Victory* with is this binnacle.' He handed a scarred brass dome to Tom. 'The damage was done by French sharpshooters at Trafalgar and this had to be replaced in the Gibraltar dockyard. It was then given to me as a memento, though I don't need any object to remind me of that glorious and tragic day.'

Sir Thomas cleared his throat and shook himself as if to clear his head of unwelcome memories. 'I said earlier that your question about rescues from wrecked ships was a good one, and it was. Have you heard of the Manby Mortar?' Tom shook his head. 'I first saw mortars used by Nelson at the battle of Copenhagen. He used bomb ketches to lob shells into the Danish fleet. Well a Captain Manby, he's an army captain by the way not navy, has adapted the naval mortar so that it can throw a line from the shore to a stranded ship. He has had some success I admit, but the whole apparatus is cumbersome and needs a crew of five or six to move it. How useful it will turn out to be I don't know. However when I was in Jamaica four or five years ago I met the C-in-C there, Admiral Charles Rowley. He had just come from commanding at The Nore in Kent where he had been asked by the Admiralty to watch the trials of something called the Trengrouse Rocket. Rowley told me this Cornishman, Henry Trengrouse, had fitted a rocket onto the end of a musket and when it fired he could shoot a line accurately for nearly 200 yards. He was very impressed and had the results written up and sent to the Admiralty recommending further trials. Rowley had no idea whether anything happened after that.' Hardy looked to see if Tom was following all this. 'So if you had had either one of Manby's mortars or Trengrouse's rockets on Portland yesterday you Coast Guards might have saved the crew of the *Arethusa*.'

Tom was fascinated and asked Sir Thomas a great number of questions. He then became embarrassed that that he might have presumed too much on the great man's time. Commodore Hardy however was impressed by his intelligence and enthusiasm. 'The main purpose, a couple of years ago, of combining the Preventive Water Guard and the Land Guard together to form the new Coast Guard Service was for greater efficiency, but the organisation is developing rapidly. It will increasingly be the task of your service to take all possible action to save lives, take charge of crippled vessels and protect property.'

'I thought our job was to stop smuggling,' Tom said.

'It is that too. But smuggling is just one small part of what the new service is for. It won't be long I'm told, before the government reduces its import taxes and when that happens I doubt if it will be worth while running contraband from France.'

Tom thought this was an ideal opportunity to raise the other problem that had been vexing him. 'I am worried that, for many people on the coast around here, the profit from smuggling is the only thing standing between them and starvation. These people seem to think there is nothing wrong in what they call free trading.'

Commodore Hardy looked at him shrewdly. 'You are quite right Tom. That is why some in authority, including one magistrate who lives not far from this house, turn a blind eye to *The Trade*. My advice to you m'boy is not to get too worked up about smuggling. Make arrests if you have to, don't take bribes yourself and concentrate on saving lives. Though you are a Riding Officer you no longer work solely for the Revenue Service. You are a member of this new Coast Guard.' He studied Tom for a while in silence. 'What do you know about sailing?' Tom admitted that his knowledge was almost non-existent. 'Pity,' Hardy said. 'If you did, I think that you would have a great future in The Service. I will see if I can put in a word for you, though I can't promise anything. I do know it is time we had some of these life saving devices here in Dorset.' He went across to an oak chest that stood in one corner and rummaged around, drawing out a leather case. 'Here is a small present for you to remember our meeting.' He handed Tom a battered leather case containing a small telescope with the initials TMH in black stamped into the leather. Tom knew these stood for Thomas Masterman Hardy. 'I have another of these somewhere. Now its time you went back to find the girls.' Tom stammered his thanks and returned to the drawing room.

Tom and Perle discovered a tipsy Jacko asleep on the grass outside the King's Arms. His face was bloodied and he had obviously been in a fight. 'One of the lads called Louisa a coarse name,' he explained. 'He won't do that again when I'm around.' Tom noticed that Perle was obviously tired and her limp was more apparent. He gently slowed his pace and the three returned to Fleet each of them, for their own reasons, content with the world.

Chapter 9
The Worst of Times

Overton liked a challenge. As with many bullies he was unsatisfied if his victim surrendered too easily. Tom Verney provided just the sort of confrontation he relished. By the boy's steadfast refusal to wash the lieutenant's clothes, Overton could justify to himself the gradual increase in torment like a medieval torturer who inch by inch turns the screw of a rack. The subtlety of his actions lay in never quite doing too much, so that he could be reported back to Bouscarle in Weymouth. He had slipped up by beating Hugh Dawkins so severely, but even then he had only received the mildest of reprimands. A fleeting worry crossed his mind. If Verney didn't crack soon, Lieutenant Overton was concerned that his authority over others in Portland might be diminished. However, this morning, when the boy reported in for work, he was pleased to see that his pinched, white face and shabby clothing suggested that his victory would not be long delayed.

During the four weeks since Tom had returned to Brandy Row and his work at the castle, he had become increasingly miserable. His pay was consistently delayed and he would not have had sufficient money to live on if it hadn't been for the generosity of the silent Matthew and further loans from Sam Ditchburn. He assumed that it was also Sam who once sent over a couple of mackerel and later some sprats, dumped on his doorstep without a word by a scruffy seven-year-old urchin. Still no other Portlander had spoken to him.

'Late again Vermin.' Overton leered at Tom, delighted to see that the recently new uniform was now stained and creased. 'Look at you. You're a disgrace to The Service. Smarten yourself up or you'll find yourself on extra parades all weekend. For now get yourself and your scrawny nag down onto Chesil. Sniff around the Fleet village and see if anything's cooking. Report back to me here and I'll give you the evening roster.'

Tom had been determined to ask Overton once again if his pay had come through, but decided against giving him the satisfaction and turned dully away to start his assignment. Ironically as Tom had grown more and more dispirited, his horse had flourished. Regular exercise, and the lush grass of the Underhill had rejuvenated him. Gussie wickered with pleasure as Tom approached. Tom scratched the tuft of hair between his ears and his horse snorted again. 'Since Hugh left you are the only one who talks to me, Gussie,' Tom said dolefully. He patted his neck and the two of them ambled off towards Chesil beach. When Tom recognised the place where he had been attacked by smugglers, he realised how much he had missed the friendship of Joby, Jacko and Perle. As the tide was out he decided to wade Gussie across the Fleet and visit Butter Street, but the front door of Number 2 was locked and there was obviously no one at home. In his present state he was desperate for any spark of kindness. He knew Joby worked less than a mile away at The Lugger Inn in Chickerell. He felt sure she would be pleased to see him.

'What do you want? We don't need no bluebottles here.' The innkeeper who barred Tom's way into the pub was far from welcoming.

'I've come to see Mrs de Bretton,' Tom said.

'She's working and your lot aren't wanted here.'

'Please can I just speak to her out here?' Tom was embarrassed by the whiney tone of his voice, but he now felt he had to see Joby.

The landlord said nothing but left Tom standing in the doorway. A few minutes later Joby came out to greet him wiping her hands on her apron. 'Isaac won't allow customs officers into his pub,' she apologised, and Tom realised that this must be the lander who had decided his fate on Chesil Beach a few weeks earlier. 'You look awful Tom. What's the matter?'

'I needed to see you or Jacko and Perle.' Tom slumped down on a pile of logs. I don't think I can go on.' He started to explain about his treatment by Overton and Joby guessed he was near to breaking.

'Perle is working for Mrs Wallace at Waddon House. She stops there now and only comes home on Sundays. I never know where Jacques is, but when he's next home, I'll tell him you asked after him. I'm sure he will come and see you on Portland.'

'Back to work Joby.' Isaac stood in the doorway with his arms folded, waiting.

'I've got to go dear.' Joby de Bretton came over to the distraught boy and planted a kiss on the top of his head. She fished in her apron pocket and pressed a silver coin into his hand. 'You look half starved, Tom. Buy yourself a decent meal.'

It was four days later when Tom returned to his little cottage that he found Jacques de Bretton waiting for him upstairs. Jacko had taken advantage of Tom's absence to snoop around and had found two letters beside his bed. Both were from Tom's sister Amanda and in the most recent she was obviously worried about him. Jacko heard Tom enter the cottage and carefully folded one of the letters and stuffed it into his pocket. He knew Perle would be interested. Despite being pre-warned by his mother, Jacko was shocked by Tom's appearance. The once smart Riding Officer was unkempt and obviously exhausted. 'Thanks for coming Jacko.' He slumped down on the straw mattress without the energy to say more.

'Ma thought you looked hungry. She's sent you one of her steak and ale pies. I left it downstairs.' Jacko quickly returned with the pie, a tin plate and two grubby spoons, which he cleaned on his shirt. Conversation was unnecessary. The two of them munched their way through Joby de Bretton's offering until the pie-dish was clean. Tom then began to tell his friend what his life had been like since they had last seen each other. 'That Overton is a right bastard,' Jacko said. 'Peaches to the smugglers whenever Bouscarle has an operation planned. He would sell his own grandmother for a couple of sovs if he thought he could get away with it.' The two young men talked late into the night but though he tried hard, Jacko failed to persuade Tom it was in his interest to swallow his pride and wash the Lieutenant's clothes.

**

Perle handed the crumpled letter back to her brother. Mrs Wallace, whose husband Major Edward Wallace

86

was the tenant at Waddon House, had given Jacko permission to speak to his sister. The two of them sat at the long pine table in the kitchen while Jacko told Perle of Tom's state of mind and unsatisfactory living conditions. 'I don't think he will manage to last out much longer,' he said. 'That turd Overton's determined to break him.' He scratched his head trying to think of something useful. 'I can't be seen going there too often. The other lads would begin to have suspicions about me.'

Mrs Wallace's entrance into the kitchen interrupted the gloomy silence. She came and sat next to Perle, asking cook to make her a cup of coffee. 'The Major wants to know if there will be another delivery soon Jacko?' Despite his two commissions, in the militia and as a magistrate, Major Wallace was a regular customer for illegal brandy and Jacko was his contact with the smugglers. Unknown to Perle, it was Major Wallace, a distant relative of the Hardy family, who had provided Joby de Bretton with the cottage in Butter Lane and persuaded Isaac to employ her at the Lugger Inn. Jacko was aware that his father had taken a young Ned Wallace on some of his trips to France and had on one occasion performed a momentous service to him, though he had no idea of the details. Neither Jacko nor Major Wallace had a scintilla of doubt that the other was completely trustworthy.

'It'll be soon, Madam. I will let the Major know when the goods are available.'

Perle decide that she and Jacko were not going to come up with any sensible suggestions and decided to outline the problem to Mrs Wallace and show her

87

Amanda's letter. Margaret Wallace was a comfortable woman to talk to, despite her lofty position as mistress of Waddon House. She regularly visited the cottages of her husband's tenants and was more content to sit in their kitchens chatting to their wives and children than she was holding tea parties in her regency drawing room. Her reputation as a fixer of problems was just the encouragement that Perle needed. 'Is this the nice young man that Louisa Hardy was telling me about? It does seem a shame that beastly Lieutenant Overton should make his life so miserable. I am only sorry the Major cannot do anything directly about this, but he has no authority over the Coast Guard.' She paused, screwing up her face in concentration, trying to work out how to overcome this knotty problem. 'Perle, Sunday is your day off. That's only four days away. You must go and tidy up his little cottage. I know Jacko can't afford to be seen with a customs official, but no one will question you. Cook will give you a basket of supplies so that the poor man doesn't starve. Jacko, you must write a letter to that sister of his. She sounds like a sensible girl and will know what to do. My brother is going back to London tomorrow and will be going through Salisbury. He will deliver it if I ask him. No more moping now. We have a plan of action and will deal with the horrid Lieutenant Overton later.' She remembered why she had come into the kitchen and gave instructions to cook about that night's supper. 'You have ten minutes to write the letter you two and then Perle must get back to work or Mrs Mossop will be after her.'

'Who's Mrs Mossop?' Jacko whispered as Margaret Wallace swept out of the kitchen.

'She's the housekeeper here. She pretends to be very fierce, but has been kind enough to me.' Cook gave them some writing paper and the two of them composed their letter to Amanda Verney.

Chapter 10
An Unlikely Commission

Perle hummed to herself as she scrubbed Tom's cooking pans. When she had arrived early at Coastguard Cottage she had been horrified both at the mess, upstairs and downstairs, and at Tom's lethargy. She knew how to deal with the mess, but Tom's lack of energy and brooding manner were outside her experience. 'You go and look after Gussie,' she told him. 'Come back in an hour and I will have some food for our lunch.' She started on the top room, bringing all the dirty crockery and stale bits of food downstairs. She struggled to open the window and managed to let in a little fresh air. A general tidy up and sweeping of the floor left the room reasonably presentable. Downstairs she cleaned out the old range and lit a fire. While a pot of stew was coming to the boil she started to work on the grease-encrusted pans. She was distracted by a knock on the front door and after carefully wiping her hands on her apron opened it.

The scene that greeted Amanda was one of apparent domestic comfort. Standing outside the door she had listened to the maid singing. Inside she found a cheerful fire blazing and the smell of stew bubbling away in a pot on the stove. 'Where is my brother?' She demanded.

Perle, who had been eagerly looking forward to Tom's return, was completely thrown by Amanda's arrival. 'He's out.' was all she could think to say. She guessed that this must be the sister who had been urgently summoned by Jacko's letter earlier in the week, but had not expected such a speedy arrival nor such a striking and confident woman.

Amanda felt far from confident. The letter signed from '*A Friend*', had been sufficiently alarming for the family conference between herself, Beth and Aunt Edith to decide that Amanda should immediately travel to Portland to see for herself what was wrong. She had taken the coach from Salisbury to Dorchester on Saturday and next day made her way by carrier to Weymouth and over the ferry to Portland. She had been directed by a surly fisherman to Brandy Lane and was steeling herself for what the letter had described as '*Tom's misery and desolation,*' only to meet with a scene that was anything but wretched. She was tired mainly from worry and her long journey but also irritated by a feeling that she had been duped. 'You can go now, girl. I will wait for my brother. He will pay you later.'

Perle tried to explain but, in her nervousness, couldn't find the right words to explain to this imposing young woman, who stood holding the door, waiting for her to leave in silence. She limped over to the stairs where she had left her cloak and left. She wondered if she should seek out Tom or stay to meet him when he returned, but decided that either of these actions might cause more of a problem with Amanda. Very confused, she decided to go back to Butter Street.

Tom was feeling slightly more himself by the time he returned home. His walk on Topside with Gussie had been good for him. He was looking forward to chatting with Perle and hoped that she would have prepared some of Joby's delicious food for lunch.

He was shocked to see his sister. 'What are you doing here?' he blurted out rudely.

'Oh Tom. It's good to see you.' Amanda went over to him and put her arms round him. 'I sent the crippled maid away and told her you would pay her later. I'll look after you today.'

Tom shook himself free. 'She's not a cripple, nor is she the maid,' he shouted at her. 'She's my friend and one of the few people who has been kind to me since I came to this awful place. What are you doing here anyhow?'

Tom had never shouted at either of his sisters before. A shocked Amanda started to cry while trying to answer his question. Tom, not interested in any explanation, dashed from the room and ran down the road into Chesilton but Perle was nowhere to be seen. When Tom returned to the house Amanda was standing where he had left her. She was no longer crying but looked whey-faced and scared. It was Tom's turn to put his arms around her and to bury his face in her shoulder. His whole body shook with sobs. Eventually the storm of his distress passed and the two of them sat down on upturned fish boxes near the fire. Amanda told him about the dreadful letter they had received and how she and Beth with Aunt Edith's help had decided she should come down to Portland. Tom told her about his life and Lieutenant Overton's systematic cruelty to him.

'Who was that girl?' his sister asked.

'That's Perle. Her brother Jacko saved my life and I expect it was the two of them who wrote the letter. They've been true friends to me. I owe them so much.'

Amanda had always been the practical one in the family and had a fine logical mind, which she now put to good use. 'Firstly we must have something to eat. Perle's food smells delicious. Where do you keep the plates?' As they ate she began to sort out Tom's various problems in her mind. 'I'll go to Perle's house and apologise for my rudeness when I can. It was only because I was tired and a little frightened that I was so abrupt. You must clean yourself up a bit Tom. You could do with a shave and your uniform needs cleaning. Tomorrow you will go to this Lieutenant and tell him you will do his washing.' Tom started to object, but his sister shushed him quiet. 'Don't be silly. It's only your pride, which is holding you back. His assault on you is making you ill and depressed. Do his washing, collect your pay and get back to a decent work schedule. When you are feeling better you can plan how you are going to get your own back. You said you thought he was taking bribes. Well then, if you find evidence you can use that against him. Remember he has the strength, you must use your brains.'

Perle had watched out for Tom's return to his cottage. Embarrassed and ashamed, she had hidden herself in the tiny side street locals humorously called No Ope, when he had come to look for her. Sadly she understood that Amanda's perception of her was right. She was just a poor kitchen maid; a servant in a big house and it was presumptuous of her to think that Tom, with all his education and knowledge, might fancy her. She now convinced herself that it was just his kind nature that had allowed him to befriend her.

Amanda's comment had shown her that even friendship with him was not possible. From her hiding place she watched Tom go back to his cottage. With a spurt of self-knowledge she realised that her hopes for a future with him had been the fanciful dreams of a lonely girl. She set off on the long walk back to her home overwhelmed by misery.

***

In the Poole customs office, Tom carefully re-read the letter which his godfather had handed to him. It was only two days since Amanda had arrived at his cottage in Portland and now his life had been turned upside down. After Amanda's sensible lecture he had reported to Portland Castle next morning looking smart and freshly shaved, having decided to make any concessions necessary to get Lieutenant Overton off his back. As soon as he had arrived, Overton had sent for him and given him a message from Arthur in Weymouth. 'Verney, you are to report straight to Captain Bouscarle's office for temporary reassignment. Luckily for you, thanks to my frequent requests, your back pay has come through.' He handed Tom a small leather bag, which chinked most satisfactorily when he shook it. 'Don't hang around. The Captain wants to see you today.' His upper lip curled in a cruel smile that Tom recognised well. 'It is only a temporary reassignment, Verney. I am already looking forward to your return.'

Tom and Amanda took the ferry over to Weymouth later that morning both wondering what had just happened. Sam had agreed to look after Gussie until his return and it did not take Tom long to pack his pitifully few belongings. 'Overton called me Verney for the first time,' he said thoughtfully. 'He also gave me all the money I was owed. He's such a devious devil. There is nothing really I can complain about,' he told Sam. 'Anything I do say will sound like whingeing.' He offered to pay back his debt to Sam, but the old man waved away the suggestion mumbling something which Tom understood to mean he should do it later.

Captain Bouscarle was away, but the oleaginous Arthur gave him a travel warrant and told him to report next day to Toby Fortescue in Poole.

Late the next morning Tom and Amanda arrived at the Poole custom's office where much to his delight the first person Tom saw was his friend Hugh Dawkins. 'What are you doing here?'

'I work here,' Hugh told him, grinning. 'I couldn't stand that awful bully any more and wanted to resign from the service, but my father persuaded Captain Fortescue to take me on here. I am now part of the Waterguard and the Number Two in a small cutter that patrols the harbour here. It's brilliant.' Tom hastily introduced Amanda to his friend and straightening his jacket, knocked on his godfather's door.

'At last you're here, Thomas. Come in and sit down. I've received this extraordinary letter.' He picked up a piece of thick paper from his desk and handed it to Tom. 'What is behind this?'

Dear Captain Fortescue,

I am instructed by his Grace the Duke of Wellington, Master General of the Ordnance to request your agreement for Thomas Verney, a Riding Officer under your command, to attend a training course at the Royal Dockyard in Portsmouth. He will receive a temporary appointment as Midshipman in his Majesty's navy and will be under naval authority for a period of at least three months. He should report to the Porter's Lodge by Victory Gate as soon as it is convenient. Midshipman Verney will return to your command on the completion of his training.

Signed   Horace Whitton
(Secretary to the Master General of Ordnance)

Tom read the short letter through twice. 'I don't know anything about this sir,' he answered. 'I did talk to Commodore Hardy in his home in Portesham. He said he would try to help my career. Perhaps it's his doing.'

Toby Fortescue tried not to show the resentment he felt at his nephew's good fortune. 'You must have made a very favourable impression on my old friend Hardy. He's no longer a commodore. It has just been announced in the *Naval Gazette* that he has recently been promoted and is now Admiral Hardy. You are a lucky young man if he is indeed your patron.' He paused as if coming to a weighty decision. 'I have determined that this will be a good opportunity for you and have given my agreement,' he said pompously. Tom secretly wondered how difficult a judgement it might be for a lowly captain of the Coast Guards to agree to a request from a newly promoted admiral and the Commander-in-chief, but wisely said nothing.

Tom left his uncle's office extremely confused by what had just happened. The Poole Comptroller of Customs handed him a travel warrant and advised him that the next stage coach to Portsmouth departed from The Antelope Inn in less than an hour's time and not to miss it. While Hugh congratulated him on his good fortune, Amanda could see that her brother was undecided if this was good news. 'You must hurry to catch the stage coach Tom,' she reassured him. 'Beth and I will be fine and I will write to your friends in Weymouth to explain what has happened.' Tom hurriedly scribbled down Perle and Jacko's names and address and with a quick kiss to his sister and a wave to Hugh he dashed down the Great Quay to find his way to The Antelope.

Chapter 11
A Great Deal to Learn

Still half asleep Tom started to count the bells. Clang clang then a pause, clang clang another pause, clang clang and a final pause followed by a single clang. He turned over in his bunk, pulling the blanket round his ears, knowing it was time to get up. Seven bells in the morning watch; that would be half past seven. He had to be on parade in half an hour. For his first few nights Tom had cursed the incessant bells that were the Royal Navy's unique method of timekeeping. But, after only eight days in the naval hostel, he already found them comforting and reassuring. In the distance he could hear the watchman at Victory Gate calling out the time and announcing, 'A fine morning and all's well!'

He had reported to the porter's lodge at the Royal Ordnance as instructed by his godfather and been directed to the office of the senior base officer, Commander Curtis. 'Welcome to Portsmouth, Midshipman Verney. I have been ordered to turn you into a sailor in as short a time as possible,' he announced. 'The next course of instruction on the lifesaving equipment doesn't start...' he looked down at the calendar on his desk... 'for two months. It usually takes five years to turn a landlubber into a naval officer but I will see what we can do in the time we have. Petty Officer Blake will be responsible for your training. Get yourself a proper naval uniform from stores. I will let you know when I wish to see you again. That will be all. Carry on.' The interview had answered only a few of the questions that crowded in on Tom, but had obviously come to an end. *Present events seemed to have a momentum of their own with very little control from me*, he thought.

Tom found his way to the stores and by liberal use of the Commander's name had managed to acquire a midshipman's uniform. From there he was directed to Gunwarf Quay where the smart little cutter called *Badger* was tied. Petty Officer Blake turned out to be nothing like Lieutenant Overton. As soon as it had been clearly established that it was he, not the newly appointed midshipman, who was in charge, the two had co-operated well together. He had worked Tom hard, first as an ordinary crewmember and then on day eight he had given him the helm for the first time. 'It's your command Mr Verney.'

Each day Tom understood how little he really knew about sailing but Blake grudgingly admitted to himself the boy was a fast learner. 'What are the two elements a sailor must always have in the front of his mind Mr Verney?'

'Wind and tide Mr Blake.'

'Quite right Mr Verney. What have we now?'

'Wind sou' by sou'west backing to south Mr Blake.' Tom held up his finger as he had seen Blake do on many occasions, 'probably force two or three.' He glanced at the rocks on Selsey Bill. 'About half tide, I should think, on the flood.' He looked up at the cutter's sails to make sure they were pulling properly and waited a little smugly for some words of praise from the petty officer. Blake said nothing. Twenty minutes later when the cutter came to a shuddering halt on the mud flats around Hayling Island Tom sheepishly corrected his earlier error. 'I believe I should have said, 'tide on the ebb,' Mr Blake.' He waited for Blake to tell him what to do next, but the petty officer was chatting to the two sailors in the well of the cutter and obviously not about their present predicament. 'Excuse me. What do we do now Mr Blake?'

'You are the officer. It's your responsibility sir.' Blake resumed his conversation with the grinning seamen.

Eight days of training isn't enough, thought Tom. *It's not fair.* But he quickly realised that Blake was not intending to help him. He would have to do something. The wind was gently pushing the cutter further onto the mud so it seemed quite a good idea to take the sails down. 'Please take in the sails Mr Blake.' Blake efficiently issued the necessary orders and the two sailors quickly furled the sails. 'We must try and shove her off the mud, back into the main channel. Please see to it Mr Blake.' Under instructions the sailors each grabbed an oar and leaning over the bows tried to move the boat, but it quickly became apparent even when Tom and Blake each picked up additional oars that the cutter was too heavy and this was having no effect. He wondered if he should order the sailors over the side to see if they could move the boat. It was unlikely this would have an effect, but at least it would wipe the smiles from their faces. Then he realised how unfair that would be. It was his mistake and his job to resolve it. 'It must be around two bells in the afternoon watch. We will have to wait here for the tide to turn. I want mudhooks fore and aft Mr Blake.' He was about to apologise to his crew for his silly mistake, but decided that this was not what an officer in the Royal Navy would do. 'It will be dark in four or five hours. Then it will be a long cold night gentlemen. Make yourself comfortable. I will take the second dog-watch and you Mr Blake you will take the first watch. Please wake me when we are afloat and find out now what food we have on board.' The petty officer sent one of the sailors below who quickly reappeared with a tin of biscuits and a bottle of what Tom suspected was French brandy that had never received the King's stamp. The four men, warmed by the brandy, eventually settled down in the tiny cabin. Tom took great pleasure in ordering Mr Blake to hand over the only blanket. *After all,* he thought, *the man could have saved us from all this if he had wanted to.*

Shortly before midnight the petty officer shook Tom awake. The two sailors were already scrambling about on deck. 'We are just about afloat Mr Verney and though the tide is flooding in there is a light land breeze which should take us through the narrows out to sea.'

Before the sun had set the previous evening Tom had taken a bearing on the entrance to Hayling Island Sound without letting Blake know. 'As soon as we are floating way the anchors and set a course sou' by sou'west if you please Mr Blake.' Under full sail they ghosted out to sea and turned west towards Portsmouth harbour. 'I have never sailed at night before Mr Blake. I would be grateful if you could take her in without any help from me.'

'Aye, aye sir,' said a relieved petty officer. It was two in the morning before the *Badger* tied up again at

Gunwarf Quay. 'Tomorrow's parade, eight o'clock as usual Mr Verney.

The next weeks were a delight for Tom. On most days Blake took him out in the *Badger* and he became increasingly confident how to handle the little cutter. The petty officer taught him many of the tricks of smugglers and though it was not strictly the navy's responsibility they did help the revenue boat arrest a French free trader. At the end of his seventh week Tom dashed down to Gunwarf Quay just before eight bells. Petty Officer Blake, smartly turned out as always, was waiting, not alongside the cutter *Badger* as was usual, but seated as coxswain in the stern of a Royal Navy longboat. There were seven sailors, none of whom had been witness to Tom's previous humiliation, sitting two to a thwart. The eighth sailor was holding the painter waiting to cast off. Blake raised a hand from the tiller in salute to Tom. 'Welcome aboard Mr Verney.' Tom scrambled down a Jacob's ladder into the boat next to Blake. 'No, Mr Verney. Your seat is in the bows next to Harris. Tom pushed his way between the rows of grinning sailors and sat down on the bow thwart next to a young man of about his own age, who he assumed was Harris. 'Up oars!' With silky smoothness seven oars were raised vertical. 'Come along Mr Verney. We don't want to disgrace the Royal Navy.' Tom found his oar lying along the gunwale and glancing over at Harris copied him by placing the butt on the thwart between his legs. 'Thank you, Mr Verney. You may cast off Martin!' The eighth member of the crew scrambled down the ladder and gave the long boat a shove away from the quay before settling in the stern next to

Blake. 'Make ready.' Tom remembered what he had learned from the lerrets of Portland and slipped his oar between the two tholepins. If Petty Officer Blake was going to try and make a clown of him Tom was determined he would be disappointed. 'Row!'

Tom stretched forward and buried his blade in the water and heaved. Unfortunately he quickly discovered that it was easier to put the heavy blade into the water than to take it out again. The oar crashed into his chest knocking him off his bench into the bow space. 'Cease rowing.' The long boat drifted into Portsmouth harbour as Tom scrambled to his feet and struggled to put his oar back in position. The crew, respecting his rank, were trying hard not to laugh, but Tom could see the humour of the situation. He grinned at Harris. 'What did I do wrong?'

'Till you've got the hang of it just take little nips at the water. The rest of us'll drive the boat.'

'Nearly set Mr Blake,' Tom called out.

'Try not to disgrace the British navy again Mr Verney. Make ready! Row!' This time Tom didn't try to prove he was the strongest man on the boat. Watching the actions of the man in front of him he took a tiny bite at the water and tried to establish himself into an easy rhythm. The boat thrashed along as gradually Tom felt he could contribute a little more effort.

'I think we're heading for Gosport and Victory,' Harris whispered out of the side his mouth. Either Blake did not hear this breach of discipline or he chose to ignore it.

In fifteen minutes just as Tom's muscles were starting to burn, Petty Officer Blake stood up in the stern. 'Ahoy, Victory. Officer on board.' Tom was ready for the next commands. 'Cease rowing. Up oars.' The long boat glided silently alongside the towering side of HMS Victory and came to a stop next to one of the companion ladders. Martin and Harris made the boat fast. 'Stow your oar and up you go Mr Verney. Don't forget to salute the quarterdeck. As Harris held the longboat fast to the rope railing, Tom stepped onto the broad wooden companion ladder. *Easy enough for even the fattest admiral to haul himself on board,* he thought. He remembered enough of Blake's instructions to give a smart salute to where he guessed Victory's quarterdeck might be and another to the naval officer who stomped over to meet him, his wooden leg making a regular thump on the wooden planks of the deck.

'Welcome aboard Victory, Mr Verney. I am Captain Arthur, commander of his Majesty's frigate Sirius until '14. He pointed to his wooden sump. 'A French canon ball dismasted me off the coast of Portugal. I am sorry you cannot see Victory in all her glory. She was a brave sight then. We have been permanently anchored here at Gosport for twelve years now and the Admiralty uses the old girl as a supply depot. Commander Curtis thought you might like to visit us. I gather you are a friend of Admiral Hardy. Of course this used to be his ship.'

Tom was beginning to realise by now that in the navy, Hardy's name opened almost any door. 'Is that Blake I can see in the longboat?' He shouted over the rail, 'Come on up Mr Blake and bring your crew with you.' He turned back to Tom. 'George Blake was a youngster here on board Victory at Trafalgar. He

104

knows this ship as well as any man alive. I can't manage the ladders with this peg of mine. He'll take you down below and show you round.'

For the next thirty minutes the petty officer showed off HMS Victory to Tom with obvious pride. As they descended deeper into the bowels of the ship Tom guessed they were well below the water line. 'This deck is called the orlop,' Blake explained. 'In my time the area we are now in was an open space called the cockpit. What are they doing filling it with cordage?' he muttered angrily. 'During the battle this is where Mr Beatty, the surgeon would operate. He pointed to a pile of ropes. 'It was here that Admiral Nelson died.'

When Tom and the petty officer returned to the main deck they found the crew of the long boat skylarking in the rigging. 'I told them they could climb the foremast,' Captain Arthur explained to Blake. 'That is the only one of the three where we've kept the sails on the yards. Next year we are expected to strip that too.'

'Would you like to climb to the top Mr Verney?' Though the foremast was considerably lower than the main mast Tom gazed upwards in horror. 'No, Mr Verney, the top is what we call that platform about one third of the way up the mast. Harris,' he called out before Tom had a chance to answer. 'Look after Mr Verney and take him to the top.'

'Aye aye, Mr Blake.' Harris gave a wicked grin to Tom. 'Follow me, Mr Verney.' Harris led Tom to what looked like a series of rope ladders rising from the deck up the foremast. 'These we call ratlines, sir.' He scampered up like a monkey. Tom noticed that unlike him, all the sailors in the rigging above had taken their shoes off the better to grip the ropes. *Too late for that now,* he thought. He put his foot onto the first rung and swung himself on to the ladder. The crew of the long boat high above him had stopped their various activities and were all watching his progress. There was no way he could back out. 'Well done Sir.' Harris slid down one of the shrouds until he was alongside Tom who envied his easy confidence. 'You're about halfway now Sir. To get to the top you can go through the lubber's hole.' Tom looked up and saw that there was just sufficient space between the mast and the wooden planking for him to squeeze through. 'We jacks always go up by the futtock shrouds.'

He swung away from Tom and scooted up again. Just below the top Tom could see a series of ropes that came from the platform at a forty-five degree angle. These must be what Harris called the futtock shrouds Tom guessed. The ropes were there to hold the platform in position but Harris was using them as his access to the top. He swung himself outwards from the ladder grabbing at one of the higher wooden slats while his feet were solid on the lowest rung. For a moment his body hung backwards over the deck but with a heave and a wriggle he pulled himself onto the platform disappearing from Tom's view. A few seconds later Harris's grinning face appeared at the lubber's hole. 'Come along, Sir. We haven't got all day.'

Afterwards Tom couldn't remember what made him decide to tackle the futtock shrouds. It could have been Harris's easy assumption that he was too scared to take the risk, or his awareness that the longboat crew were all watching and assessing him or even a wish to prove himself to Petty Officer Blake. Whatever the reason when he arrived at the decision point he launched himself outwards as he had seen Harris do, grabbing at one of the cross rungs. His feet scrabbled for the nearest wooden slat, but his shoes slipped and he found himself hanging in space thirty feet above the deck of HMS Victory. He tried to swing his legs inwards but however he twisted his body he could not get either of his feet into position.

'Hang on Mr Verney.' Tom was conscious that Harris had scrambled back through the lubber's hole. Clinging with one arm onto one of the shrouds he grabbed at Tom's leg and hauled it towards one of the rungs. With his feet firmly positioned Tom felt a little more secure but his arms were already tiring. 'Better come back to the mast, Sir,' Harris advised him, but Tom reckoned it was almost as dangerous to go back as to go on forwards. He hauled himself up one more rung but still had to manoeuvre himself over the lip of wooden platform. 'Grab hold of my hand Sir.' Later Tom discovered that Harris had whistled up two other crewmembers from the longboat. He was unceremoniously hauled onto the top by his arms and trousers where he laid floundering and gasping like a fish newly landed on the beach. Harris's anxious face appeared through the lubber's hole. 'Better get to your feet, Sir. Show the captain that you are all right.'

Harris is more concerned about my dignity than I am, he thought. *I suppose it's important for the sailors to be able to respect their officers.* He struggled to his feet clinging onto the mast with one arm and giving a half-hearted wave to the watchers below with the other.

The two sailors, who had helped Tom, had disappeared along the giant spar, which ran out at right angles to the mast. The folded sail seemed to provide a secure enough footing for them, but Tom was not tempted to follow. *I've managed to escape from one foolish decision, better not risk a second.* At the end of the spar, which Tom knew was called the yardarm, the two of them grabbed hold of ropes and slid to the deck. Tom took off his shoes and tied them round his neck. He then carefully picked his way through the lubber's hole and slowly climbed down the Jacob's ladder. 'Thank you. That was most interesting.' Tom bowed slightly to Captain Arthur. Petty Officer Blake looked at him quizzically but said nothing.

Back in the launch Blake beckoned Tom to a seat in the stern. 'You take us back to Gunwarf Quay Mr Verney.' Tom had taken note of the sequence of orders when they had departed that morning. He was about to order the sailors to cast off from Victory when a wicked idea came to him. 'Harris. You come and sit next to me. You take Harris' place please, Mr Blake.' Blake looked up startled and was about to object when he noticed the rest of the crew waiting expectantly for his reaction. He had given command to Tom and had no option but to take the empty space on the bow thwart. 'Cast off! Up oars! Make ready! Row.' Tom could see that Blake was making a very creditable showing, but could not resist one more little jab. 'Keep time please Mr Blake. The whole of Portsmouth is watching us.'

The Petty Officer hadn't lost his skill. The little boat danced over the water and Tom carefully and accurately brought her alongside the quay. 'Thank you Mr Verney,' Blake said to him. I needed the exercise. Now you report to Commander Curtis at the end of the first dog watch.' Tom was left wondering if his little joke had been taken rather badly.

Exactly on six o'clock Tom knocked on the Commander's door. Curtis was sitting behind a solid looking oak desk and immediately invited Tom to sit. 'I have here Petty Officer Blake report on your progress over the last two months. From tomorrow you will no longer call yourself a midshipman.

Tom's stomach lurched and he found it hard to disguise his disappointment. He knew he had made mistakes, but he had tried hard to live up to the confidence Admiral Hardy had shown in him. Curtis hadn't finished. 'What is your opinion of Blake?'

Despite what must have been a damning report, Tom had had time to think about Blake's methods. He realised he had been given a unique opportunity to see the navy at close hand. 'I think he is a fine instructor sir. He gave me a huge range of experiences and I regret that I have let him down. The fault is mine not his.'

Commodore Curtis looked up at Tom and for the first time smiled. 'I think you have misunderstood what I have been saying Mr Verney. I shall read part of Blake's report to you.

Though totally inexperienced in matters of the sea, Mr Verney learned quickly. He showed courage and initiative and most important he learned from his mistakes. The crew liked and respected him. Given different circumstance he would have made a fine naval officer who I would have been proud to serve under.

'There is more; some details of what you have been up to, but Petty Officer Blake has given you a glowing report. Though you will continue to wear the uniform of a naval midshipman, from tomorrow you will have a commission as Chief Boatman in the Coast Guard Service. He held up a letter, which Tom could see had various seals and embossements. 'If it is my opinion that you have completed the first part of your training successfully, I am authorised to give you this.' He handed the letter across to Tom. 'Report to the gunnery sergeant outside the armoury at eight bells tomorrow morning.'

Chapter 12
Guns and Things

A few minutes before eight next morning Tom arrived outside the Armoury to join an odd group of four men in a motley of naval uniforms. He seemed to be the youngest by a great many years. One, Tom guessed by his uniform he was a naval lieutenant, stamped his feet and blew on his fingers to try and keep warm. He nodded to Tom and moved as if to speak to him, but was constrained by the silence of the others. A second, an older man, appeared to have lost an arm if the empty jacket sleeve pinned across his chest was good evidence. As the bells struck for eight o'clock the door of the Armoury opened and out stepped the gunnery sergeant. Tom had never seen him before, but it could be no other. He silently surveyed his pupils. At least six foot six with an extra eight inches for the magnificent shako on his head he towered over the others. 'My name is Gunnery Sergeant Killerton.' He paused and let the silence drag out as he surveyed his students. 'The uniform I wear is that of the Royal Artillery and you will see from the device on my cap badge,' he pointed to a small brass plate on the shako, 'that the Royal Artillery is controlled by the Board of Ordnance not the War Office. The difference is important. I have been asked to come down here from Woolwich to teach you sailors,' (he was able to pour considerable scorn into that one word), 'something about mortars and rockets.' He smoothed the waxed ends to his considerable moustache as if to reassure himself that everything was still in its right place. 'Though my name is Gunnery Sergeant Killerton, throughout your training you will call me 'Guns.' Is that clear?' There was a mumbled response from the five men assembled in front of him. 'I said...IS THAT CLEAR?' His voice was as hard as ice.

'Yes, Guns.' This time the response was loud and together.

'Now who have we here.' He looked at the board he had been holding in his left hand. 'Captain Warburton?'

'Yes Guns.'

'Captain Warburton is watch commander of the Scarborough station. Captain Warburton would like us to believe that he lost his arm fighting the Spanish in the Caribbean, but in truth he lost it after a catfight in a Georgetown whorehouse. Isn't that right Captain?'

Warburton, who had plenty of experience dealing with NCOs like the gunnery sergeant, smiled back. 'If you say so Guns.'

'Lieutenant Brigstock?'

'Yes Guns.' The miserable looking man of about 35, who had nearly spoken to Tom on his arrival, looked mournfully towards the sergeant.

'Lieutenant Brigstock is from the Deal Coast Guard station and his naval career was so distinguished that he failed his lieutenancy exams six times.'

'Five times. I passed on the sixth,' he replied with a little show of spirit.

'Five times...what?'

'Five times, Guns.'

Killerton looked down at his list. 'Midshipman Verney.'

'Yes Guns.'

'Mr Verney is from the Portland watch station. I know he doesn't look old enough to be out without his nanny, but I am told that yesterday he ordered one of the navy's senior petty officers to row across Portsmouth harbour, so he can't be all bad.'

'It wasn't like that Guns.' Tom felt he needed to give some sort of explanation.

'Say nothing more Mr Verney. In The Red Lion last night I was bought several drinks on the strength of your exploit.' He looked back down at his list. 'Lieutenants Gurney and Mercer?'

'Yes Guns.' The remaining two officers replied together.

'Both of you are from the Port of London, and both with some naval experience of gunnery. I don't expect you will have a great deal of need for rescue equipment in London, but we will do our best to train you none the less. Now gentlemen, follow me.'

Guns marched them from the main entrance to the armoury round the side of the building and in through some double doors. He carefully removed his magnificent headgear and hung it on a peg, replacing it with a round, royal blue cap. He then led his group over to a wooden crate roughly four feet square, which was guarded by a young private from the Royal Artillery. From a rack he collected two carrying poles and slipped them through reinforced holes in the top of the box. He summoned two orderlies to assist and then ordered all the younger members of his class to follow him again, this time carrying the box. The one-armed captain, still smiling, followed along behind. The little troop staggered across the grass down to the quayside, there relieved to be able to put down their load. Guns fussed around the box, moving it two feet to the left and turning it through ninety degrees. 'In here gentlemen we have the recent invention of Captain Manby of the Norfolk militia.' He unpinned four catches at the top corners of the box and lowered the hinged sides. 'This mortar comes with its own gun platform.'

Tom had never seen a cannon like it before. It was small and black but looked mean and deadly. The barrel, short and snub-nosed, tilted upwards at about 60 degrees. It was held in position by a ratchet wheel. The breech was wide enough to hold a six-pound cannon ball. In the box with the mortar there were two canon balls each with a metal handle welded to it attached to a short chain, some bags of gunpowder and a length of slow match. The gunnery sergeant told his pupils to watch and learn as he carefully unpacked the various items from around the mortar and laid them on the wooden platform.

'Whereas the cannon fires its ball directly at the target, the mortar lobs its missile up in the air in a carefully measured arc. Admiral Nelson, one of the few intelligent sailors of recent years, used bomb ketches armed with mortars in the Baltic in 1801. He was able to destroy a Danish fleet by lobbing bombs over the pebble banks they were hiding behind, but of course the army has used mortars for years to send explosives over defensive walls. Pay attention all of you.' He picked up one of the bags of gunpowder and weighed it carefully in his hand before putting it down the barrel of the mortar. He then followed this with one of the cannon balls. 'It is important to leave the chain outside as it is to this you will secure your line.' He gave the ratchet a couple of turns to raise the elevation of the barrel, tested the wind strength and direction and then lowered the ratchet back to its original position. 'Now Mr Verney, please go and place your hat over there on the lawn. Tom walked a hundred and fifty yards towards the buildings and dropped his hat on the grass. Guns signalled that he was to move it a little to the left and a few yards further out which he did.

By the time Tom re-joined the group, Guns was blowing on a glowing length of flax cord called a slow match. The mortar was pointing directly towards Commander Curtis's office window. 'Don't you think you are taking a risk shooting at the building, Guns?' Lieutenant Mercer asked nervously.

'I'm taking no risk at all, Lieutenant.' Killerton said cheerfully. 'You're the one who is going to fire this shot. Now stand back the rest of you. Mr Mercer, you stand to the side.' He handed Mercer the slow match and the lieutenant gingerly applied it to the touch-hole.

The six pound shot, with chain flying behind, gracefully wooshed into the air and landed on the lawn a hundred and fifty yards away to roll gently forward until it was nestling next to Tom's hat.

'How did you do that Guns?' Tom asked in awe.

'How do you think lad?'

'I watched you carefully. You calculated the amount of powder needed, the wind direction and speed and the elevation of the cannon and from these worked out where the shot would land.'

'Tell him Captain Warburton.'

The Captain smiled his slow smile. 'You've done it before Guns; probably hundreds and hundreds of times so you know exactly where the ball will end up. All your little tweaks and gestures were just to impress us. They meant nothing.'

'Thank you, Captain. By the time we have finished in two weeks time you will all be able to set up the necessary tackles, load and fire this little beauty blindfolded. Very few ships run aground in a light breeze in the middle of the day. As coastguards you will need to use the rescue equipment at night in the strongest of storm winds. Now collect your hat and the missile Mr Verney.'

During the next ten days Tom learned about tackle called endless whiplines and running blocks. He was a good student and quickly understood the reason for Guns' insistence on methodical preparation and good order. Should the various ropes and lines become entangled during a rescue the whole effort would be wasted. Day by day more and more items were added to the mortar box. The little squad drilled and drilled until each of them could fire the mortar and send the line to a potentially stricken vessel as a matter of routine.

***

'This morning we are going to forget about Captain Manby's little brainchild and learn about Mr Henry Trengrouse's contribution.' The group of students had shrunk to four as Lieutenant Gurney had left for home. Guns refused to say why, but the young man

116

had shown little aptitude or interest in learning and Tom expected that both instructor and student were pleased that he had gone. The gunnery sergeant held out a standard army musket. Beneath the barrel was a small cylinder fastened on with two rings in place of a bayonet. 'Into this Mr Trengrouse has instructed me to place a small rocket.' He pulled a packet out of his knapsack and ripped off the greased paper wrapping slipping the rocket into the cylinder. 'To this I attach a light line.' While he spoke he carried out his own directions and when he had finished he held the musket out for his students to see. 'You will see that for now I am using the standard flintlock firing mechanism. Throughout the army this will soon be superseded by the percussion cap which should be much more efficient for your purposes.'

He then pointed the musket into the air and pulled the trigger. It took a while for the flint spark to light the gunpowder, but when it did the rocket sailed up into the sky trailing the fine cord behind it. The rocket seemed to cover the same distance as the mortar missile. 'Now which is better Captain Manby's invention or Mr Trengrouse's?' A lively discussion followed. Tom argued that the rocket was better suited to somewhere like Portland as it was lighter to carry to where it was needed and the line could be recovered if it missed its target first time. Captain Warburton preferred Manby's mortar as the heavier cannon ball was less likely to deviate in strong winds and weather conditions would most likely be poor when the equipment was needed.

'Any coast guard station should have both,' Guns answered his own question. 'There will be occasions when each will prove to be the right choice. Once you have become experienced with the rocket, this course is ended. Tomorrow you will all go home. The Ordnance Department will send equipment for both the mortar and the rocket to each of your watch stations. I shall return to Woolwich. You may collect your travel warrant from the Porter's Lodge. Good luck gentlemen. Let me know how you get on.' Gunnery Sergeant Killerton saluted, turned smartly on his heel and left.

Chapter 13
A New Start

Tom stood in front of Captain Bouscarle. His experiences in the Ordnance School, the positive reports from Petty Officer Blake and Gunnery Sergeant Killerton and above all the resilience of a healthy young man gave him a self-confidence that had been entirely lacking the previous occasion he had faced his commanding officer. Without comment he handed across the certificate of his appointment as Chief Boatman and the letter of recommendation from the base commander at Portsmouth.

'Er, well done Verney!' Bouscarle could see no positive outcome from Tom's promotion. He would have to find more pay for the young man on an already stretched budget. Eventually head office would supply the arrears, but for several months he and Arthur would have to scrape the extra funds from somewhere. Above all he would have to deal with Saul Overton. He found it difficult to manage Overton's hectoring, bullying manner and avoided contact with him as much as possible. Saul would not be pleased by Tom's promotion.

Tom now realised that his commanding officer was a weak man. Previously he had thought of him as a kind, overworked officer, but with his newfound confidence he recognised in Bouscarle a timid shell of a man whose actions were motivated more by self-preservation than by any moral considerations. Lieutenant Overton controlled him by the aggressive use of a powerful and unpleasant personality. Arthur managed him by the subtle misuse of his position as comptroller. If Tom's position was to improve he would have to learn to manage Captain Bouscarle too.

'There were some problems over my pay before I left for Portsmouth,' Tom told him. 'I hope your office will manage to sort this out. Please will you check with Arthur?'

The weasely comptroller, who had obviously been listening at the door, was well aware of Saul Overton's little games with the pay of men under him. 'Mr Verney has a little back pay due Sir, from the time before the navy began to pay him.' He handed Tom an envelope with some notes in it.

'Thank you Arthur.' Tom was not going to stand back and let himself be trodden on. 'Please make certain that the right amount is sent weekly to Lieutenant Overton. I am sure I can trust on the effectiveness of this office.' Despite Arthur's unctuous manner and twisted morality Tom reckoned he ran this end efficiently.

'Have you told Mr Verney about his visitor, sir?'

'Thank you, Arthur. I had forgotten.' Bouscarle turned to Tom. 'A Mrs de Bretton called in shortly after you left. She was very concerned about you and said some,' he hesitated trying to find the right word, '...er forthright remarks about Lieutenant Overton. She was greatly relieved to hear that you were well and had gone to Portsmouth.'

'May I call in at her house before I return to Portland sir?'

'Yes, yes.' Bouscarle was anxious to see the back of Tom as soon as possible, but Tom was not yet finished.

'I would think you would like to reassure yourself as to my competence as Chief Boatman sir. Perhaps tomorrow we could go out together in *The Georgia* and sail to Portland Castle? You could let Lieutenant Overton know in person of my new position, particularly in regards to the new lifesaving equipment that will soon be delivered. As the only trained officer I assume I am to be in charge.'

Bouscarle once again felt cornered and as usual took the line of least resistance. 'Yes of course you are.' The letter on his desk was quite clear on that point. 'Very well then. Meet me on *The Georgia* at nine o'clock tomorrow morning. I will see what you have learned.'

***

Joby de Bretton studied Tom with her flour-stained arms on hips. 'You look well enough. We were all worried about you. Perle was upset that she didn't have a chance to say goodbye to you. That Mr Bouscarle said you had gone to Portsmouth and didn't know how long you would be away. Though he means well he's about as useful as a rotten mackerel.' She rattled along like a runaway carriage hardly taking time to draw breath.

'Can I spend the night here Joby?' Tom at last had time to squeeze in a question.

She happily agreed and then answered his next questions. 'Jacques has gone over to France to stay with his father's family for a while. He says he is there to learn a trade, but I fear for him what that trade might be. Perle is still at Waddon House and doing very well. Mrs Wallace thinks very highly of her. You will see her tonight.' In fact Perle was not due to visit her mother until the weekend, but Joby knew she would never be forgiven if she let Tom escape without telling Perle that he was spending the night in Butter Street. 'Make yourself comfortable here. I have to go to work at *The Lugger* until seven o'clock, but I will be back in time to cook your supper.' She quickly finished off decorating a meat pie. Then dusting off her hands she slipped into her coat, kissed him on the cheek and left. Tom felt lost at first, but quickly decided that he had nothing else pressing to do and might as well relax in the little cottage where he did feel quite at home.

Isaac, the landlord of The Lugger was reluctant to give Joby the time off to visit Waddon House as she requested. He grumbled that he was as usual short staffed but, as he also had a message for Major Wallace, agreed that his young son should go. 'Tell Perle that Tom will be staying the night at home,' she told young Ben.

Isaac's message was less direct. 'The Major needs to hear that there will be another delivery next week. He is to let me know if he has any requirements.' Ben said he understood both messages and ran off. Joby settled down to her evening's work.

Tom scrambled from the armchair as the small hurricane that was Perle burst into the room. She flung her arms round him almost knocking the surprised boy off his feet. 'I was so worried about you,' she mumbled with her head buried into the front of his jacket. We didn't know what had happened to you.'

Tom patted her shoulder, as he would have comforted Amanda or Beth when they had hurt themselves. In response Perle wriggled her head even closer into his jacket. Tom discovered that he enjoyed having her body pressed against his and was in no hurry to draw himself away. The nearest part of her that he could reach was the top of her head, which he gently kissed. To his confusion Perle burst into tears and pulled away from him. She looked up at him with an angry, tearstained face. 'Why didn't you tell us where you had gone?' she said and rushed forward to bury her face once again in his jacket.

Tom remembered guiltily that the last occasion he had seen Perle was during his depressed time, when she had come to help him in his cottage on Brandy Row. Belatedly he realised that she would have been hurt by his sister's comments and regretted that he had not taken the opportunity to put things right. He vaguely remembered having asked Hugh or his sister to send a message back to the de Bretton family, but he had never taken the trouble to find out whether either of them had done so. He peeled Perle off him and held her by the shoulders at arms length. 'Perle I am truly sorry. I was very unwell when you last saw me, but that doesn't excuse my neglect of you and your mother who have always been very kind to me. I should have let you know how I was. I guess it was you and Jacko who sent for Amanda and I thank you for your thoughtfulness. I am fully recovered now and have come back to Portland to work.' He pulled Perle close to him. In the months he had been away she had tried to forget about him, but without success. Now her little storm had blown itself out and she leaned her head against him once more with a contented sigh. Tom realised that by his action he had made an unspoken commitment to Perle. To his surprise he found that this pleased him. When Joby returned she found the fire blazing, Perle working away cooking supper at the range and the two of them chatting over Tom's experiences in Portsmouth.

Next morning Tom stood in the stern of *Georgia* waiting for Captain Bouscarle to arrive. There were six crewmembers in the well of the boat. The Georgia was considerably larger than *The Badger* he had worked with at Portsmouth but he was confident he could manage. He remembered Petty Officer Blake's dictum and spoke to the coxswain who was standing next to him. 'What's the state of wind and tide?'

'Little enough wind here in the harbour sir. Gentle breeze from the southwest when we get into the bay. Ebb tide, wanting two hours to low water. Should be able to get clear of the river mouth without needing the sweeps.' This gave Tom all the information he needed. He hoped the captain would allow him to take *Georgia* out to sea. He was felt sure he could manage it with the help of what looked like an experienced crew. If he didn't take this chance to impress Captain Bouscarle he might never have another opportunity

'Care to take her out Mr Verney?' Captain Bouscarle asked as he stepped over the rail into the well.

'Aye aye sir. After his weeks on *Badger* the naval response came naturally to Tom. 'Make sure the sheets are loose and then hoist the sails. Stand by to cast off. Push her bows into the current, sailor. Take her down the middle of the stream please Coxswain.' Tom rattled off the orders with apparent confidence and the *Georgia* slipped away from the quayside with her bows being dragged round by the ebbing tide. As the lugger cleared Nothe Point the sails filled and the boat sprang to life and headed across Weymouth Bay.

'Where are you heading Mr Verney?'

'I thought I would take her out into the bay for a while sir just to get the feel of the wind. Then I will take her over to Portland Castle. I expect you will want to talk to Lieutenant Overton about my position.' Tom had already realised that it was not a difficult manoeuvre to get to Castle Quay which was lying almost directly head to wind, but he wanted to make it a smooth as he could. He brought *Georgia* in confidently enough alongside *Samphire* and let the sails flap while a crewmember made her fast. 'Perhaps I could take her out on a short patrol sir, while you are talking to Lieutenant Overton.'

'Very well, Mr Verney. Don't be more than an hour,' Bouscarle said testily. He knew he was again being managed, but he had no particular wish for Tom to be present at this meeting with Saul Overton. Such encounters had rarely been comfortable or dignified affairs in the past.

Tom let the coxswain take *Georgia* out from the quay and decided to patrol the east coast of Portland. The boat pottered gently along not far from the shore protected by the cragged cliffs. The coxswain named each of the bays and headlands to Tom who saw them from the sea for the first time. 'There's Rufus castle,' he said pointing at a ruin on the skyline. After this comes Freshwater Bay and we ought to turn there before we come to The Bill sir. It will be rough on The Race with this tide.'

As they looked into the bay a small rowing boat scuttled towards the shore as two men pulled frantically at the oars. 'Looks like Jed Homer and his brother,' the coxswain muttered. 'I expect there'll be more tubs down there, Sir.'

Tom looked through the glass and saw half a dozen barrels stacked in the stern of the rowing boat. 'Too far off to identify the villains. Do we have any creeping irons on board Coxswain?'

'That we do sir.' The coxswain grinned at Tom and issued a stream of orders to the crew. Tom knew that while they might be reluctant to identify individual smugglers, the crew would be delighted to recover any smuggled goods and to take their share of the bounty.

The coxswain manoeuvred the Georgia under sweeps towards the marker buoy conveniently left where Tom had first spotted the little rowing boat. The creeping iron was a long shanked implement with five prongs something like a kedge anchor. While the sweeps gently moved the lugger along the coxswain cast the creeping iron over the stern and let it drag along the seabed.

'I think I've snagged something, Sir,' he reported and up popped a couple of tubs to bob on the surface just over Georgia's stern. The next pass released four more tubs with two more on a third pass. One of the crewmembers, not busy on the sweeps, cheerfully hooked the floating barrels on board as they drew along side. They had no luck on the next two passes. 'I think that's our lot Sir. Perhaps we ought to be reporting back to the captain. We've had our full hour,' the coxswain suggested.

Back at Castle Quay, Bouscarle was irritated with Tom over his lateness, but brightened up when he saw the contraband stowed in the bows and accepted Tom's explanation. 'Were you able to arrest anyone?

'No sir.' Tom could feel the tension among the crew. 'The villains were too far away to make identification possible and they made good their escape on shore.' He felt there was no need to mention the coxswain's tentative identification of the Homer brothers. He briefly wondered whose side he was on.

Chapter 14
The Gun Crew

Overton was not waiting on the quayside. Tom wasn't expecting congratulations on his promotion or even a let up of the usual stream of sarcasm and venom, but nor was he particularly concerned about their first meeting. Weeks at Portsmouth had taught Tom a great deal more about himself and how to deal with his fellow man than all his years in grammar school. He accepted that, for reasons he didn't fully understand, Saul Overton was likely to be his enemy. He would first learn to manage him, and then when the time was right he would get even with him.

Lieutenant Overton was surprisingly affable when Tom arrived at his office. 'Welcome back, Verney (*not Vermin Tom noticed*). I hear you are Number Two in this watch station now. Don't let it go to your head, boy. I remain in charge here.' He paced around the narrow room as if uncertain how to make his next move. 'Tell me about this life saving equipment. What is so special about it?'

Tom gave an honest and straightforward account of the training on the Manby mortar and the Trengrouse rocket. 'These should be delivered within the next few weeks. I will then need to train up a team of helpers and I hope we will manage to save some lives next time there is a wreck on Portland.'

'These weapons should be locked away here in the castle armoury. We don't want the local rabble stealing them. I expect that you will want to move into the Castle now we have space for you.'

Tom had anticipated both these suggestions. There was no way he was going to surrender his freedom and come and live under Overton's suspicious eye. 'The mortar is extremely heavy and we are recommended to store it as close to where it might be needed as we can. It is most likely that wrecks will be on the west coast of the island or on Chesil beach. I would suggest we make a secure store in my house in Chesilton. I should remain there to keep and eye on it.'

It was such a sensible suggestion that Overton could not immediately think of a reason to counter this. 'There's no money available to pay your helpers. You will have to scrape together whatever dross you can.'

Whatever his reasons, for the time being Saul Overton had decided not to challenge Tom who was confident that, when the time came, he would be able to find plenty of volunteers among the young men of Portland. As for payment, he could promise them a share of any reward there might be for saving lives. He left Overton's office well pleased with himself. Without confrontation, he had managed to secure the first two of his objectives and no mention of laundry. He hoped he had laid sufficient groundwork with Arthur to receive his pay regularly. Once he had his team trained, his next campaign would be to get Overton's consent to take out *Samphire*. Regular anti-smuggling patrols would cut down the ease with which illegal goods came into Portland and he would enjoy the sailing.

***

That evening in The Cove House Inn, Tom sat having a friendly pint of beer with Sam Ditchburn. The first thing Tom did was to repay the money he had borrowed from Sam and which had kept him fed at the time he was at his lowest. Sam reported that Gussie was in good health. He had lent the horse to a local quarryman who had injured his leg in a rock fall some weeks ago and Tom's apparent generosity, even though he had known nothing about this, meant he was held in high regard in the village.

'I hear that Lieutenant Hendrick's men picked up Jed and Zac Homer this morning with four half-ankers of best Hollands,' Sam told him.

Tom was unsure if Sam was telling him or fishing for further information. *Probably a bit of both,* he thought. 'What will happen to them?' he asked.

'I 'spect they'll come before Dorchester beaks next week. Then it'll be either a fine or some days inside. Four half-ankers is hardly serious smuggling. No one was injured, but I did heart Jed cursing that Overton and swearing to get even with him.'

'What had Lieutenant Overton to do with it?' Tom asked.

'He had promised the boys that in the morning there would be no revenue cutters out on that stretch. When they saw the *Georgia* come into Freshwater Bay they panicked and changed their plans. They were intending to leave the catch hidden on the beach, but they thought Overton had double-crossed them for the bounty and would land a crew to capture them.'

There were at least six half-ankers I saw in the rowing boat, Tom thought. 'I expect they will have a little something set aside to pay the fine,' he said to Sam. The old man looked quizzically at Tom, nodded and smiled.

The rest of the evening Tom spent telling Sam Ditchburn about his training in Portsmouth and his plans for a rescue station on Portland. Sam reckoned he would be able to find five or six young men who would be interested to make up a volunteer crew and promised to ask around. They agreed that there was nothing to be done until the equipment arrived.

The next few weeks passed as a period of calm for Tom. Perle made a regular Sunday visit and the two of them explored the island together and became more and more comfortable in each other's company. Number 4 Brandy Row was now called Coast Guard Cottage. One weekend Perle brought over some carpentry tools and the two of them used timber from the beach to make one of the outhouses at Coast Guard Cottage into a secure store for the mortar. Tom carried out his work conscientiously regularly patrolling the west coast of the island and largely keeping out of Overton's way. He guessed that Captain Bouscarle's intervention had made a difference. Overton was prepared to wait for Tom to make a mistake. When that happened he would use his authority to bring trouble.

Some five weeks after Tom's return to the island one of the young fishermen called Mikey hurried over to the Castle to find Tom. He had heard that a carter was coming across on the ferry with a heavy crate sent from the collector in Weymouth to Portland Castle. Tom returned immediately to Chesilton with Mikey. He had no wish for Lieutenant Overton to get his hands on his equipment. If that happened it might be locked in the castle armoury forever. Fortunately, to Tom's surprise, the crate was addressed to a Senior Boatman Verney and he was able to divert the carter to his cottage and with Mikey's help the three of them carried it into the secure storeroom behind Tom's quarters.

Mikey was only sixteen but was determined to be one of Tom's rescue crew. He told Tom that when Sam had first mentioned the idea in the snug bar there were plenty of his friends who wanted to join. He helped Tom unpack the crate and gazed in awe at the new snub-nosed canon that was revealed. There were three of Manby's adapted cannon balls, a small keg of gunpowder and a long length of cord packed round the mortar. To Tom's regret there were none of Trengrouse's rockets. 'Tell your friends to meet me in the snug of The Cove at 6.00 tonight,' he told Mikey. Then, to avoid any awkward confrontation, he went back over to the castle to let Lieutenant Overton know about the delivery.

After the fishing boats had landed their catch next morning, Tom and his little group of volunteers trudged along the pebbles of Chesil beach carrying their special box. Sam Ditchburn had helped Tom select his volunteers and suggested that Nathaniel Cropper, who with his younger brother Cad was one of the chosen five, would make an excellent second in command. Tom divided his troops into two squads. Nat with Ted White and Mikey would be responsible for all ropes and harnesses while Tom with the help of Cad Cropper and Abe Senior would be responsible for the gun. Apart from the 16-year-old Mikey all the young men were around Tom's age. The little party trekked along the beach until they were clear of the final fishing boat. With only three of the special missiles to play with, Tom was determined not to waste any of them by firing out to sea. He explained to the troop how the painted arrow on the box indicated the direction the mortar was facing and with considerable excitement they unpacked and loaded it for the fist time. Tom had taken the trouble to weigh out several canvas cartridges of gunpowder. He was confident he could fire the gun, but less sure where the missile would end up. Remembering the gunnery sergeant's demonstration he told Mikey to go and place his cap 150 yards away on the crest of the pebble bank. He made sure that the little chain was hanging outside the barrel showing Nat where the line would be attached for a rescue and instead tied to it an old piece of white rag.

As soon as Mikey returned Tom applied the slow match to the touch-hole and with a satisfying swoosh the cannon ball was launched skywards trailing its little white banner. Tom did not yet have the experience of Sergeant Killerton and had obviously been at fault somewhere in his calculations. As the ball started its descent it was obvious that it would overshoot Mikey's cap by over 50 yards. To Tom's mortification it came down in the shallow waters of the Fleet and sank into the mud. Only the little white flag was left visible. Tom started to make his apologies to his crew, but quickly saw that to them the demonstration had been a huge success. Mikey and Cad splashing around in the lagoon had soon retrieved the cannon ball and brought it back triumphantly to reunite it with the mortar. Tom decided to raise the barrel a couple of notches for their next shot and this time he allowed Cad to apply the match. There was a great cheer as the gun fired and a second cheer when the ball was seen to settle remarkably close to Mikey's cap.

Tom demonstrated to Nat, Mikey and Ted the importance of driving the metal spikes deep into the pebbles to make a secure anchor point for the ropes and for the third firing Tom allowed them to attach a thin line to the cannon ball first making sure the other end was securely tied to the base.

'What do you do when you have the line on board?' Sam Ditchburn with a crowd of small children had wandered over to watch the demonstration and his question was one that Tom was uncertain how to answer.

'I suppose the crew will use it to haul over a thicker rope and we will drag one of the ship's boats safely to shore with the crew on board.'

'In the surf we get in Deadman's Cove the boat would probably capsize,' Sam said thoughtfully. 'It's likely no one would be saved. What you need is a couple of blocks and an endless whip.' He explained to the group how, if this double line could be dragged out to the stricken vessel, individual crewmembers could be hauled over one by one without losing the connection between boat and shore. 'Come back to my shed and I'll show you what I mean.'

The crew helped Tom pack up the mortar and carry it back to the Cove House Inn. It quickly became apparent how useful it was to have fishermen to work with. Nat quickly grasped Sam suggestions and the two of them were able to demonstrate to the others what Sam had meant by an endless whip. 'If we tie a rope round the man we are rescuing, isn't there a danger we will crush his chest?'

'Why don't we sit him in a chair?' Mikey said. There was general laughter at this ridiculous image, but Nat seized on the idea. 'You're right Mikey. We could make a chair out of one of these old lobster pots. It will be light but should be strong enough to stand up to a battering by the waves.'

'We could attach cork to the bottom so that it will float if it gets dunked in the sea,' Abe suggested. The idea met with general approval. 'My uncle makes pots and I could tell him what we want. Like a lobster pot, but open at the top so that a man could climb in, and two holes in the bottom for his legs to hang out.'

Abe was commissioned to ask his uncle to make what Nat called the Portland Rescue Pot and promised Tom he would collect sufficient rope and tackle to make the endless whip.

'Next time we practise with the ropes and blind folded,' Tom told them. 'I want to be able to fire the mortar accurately in pitch black with a gale blowing. But well done today. It's been a good start.'

Chapter 15
An Unexpected Break

The snug bar of The Cove House Inn was these days a more welcoming place than when Tom had first come to the island. He was glad to escape the cold and damp of a dreary March evening and was looking forward to a pint of local ale. A couple of the young men playing dominoes called out to him and he waved an acknowledgement. Sam Ditchburn had sent him a message asking for an urgent meeting and Tom found him at his usual table in the corner. The old man was puffing at his pipe and signalled to the girl to bring over a drink for Tom. Sam said nothing as they waited.

'Pint of your usual Master Tom?'

'Thanks, Annie.' Tom took a long pull at his beer. 'Now, Sam, what's this urgent meeting about?'

Sam took his time in answering. He looked at Tom weighing up how best to pass on the information. 'People here trust you lad. You do your job, and they respect you for that, but you don't go out of your way to get local folk into trouble.' He paused to pick up his pint mug and appeared to study the beer before putting it down again. 'I've a message for you from Jed Homer. I told him proper you wouldn't waste the knowledge.'

Tom knew better than to try and hurry the old man. 'Jed and Nat are back from Dorchester then? I'm pleased about that.'

'Jed said to tell you that your boss, that Saul Overton, would be meeting someone he shouldn't in Tout Quarry. He thought you should know, but he doesn't want t'other man in any trouble.' He paused and looked at Tom waiting for some response.

'I see no need to involve anyone else. If the Lieutenant is doing something wrong then he is the one I'm interested in.'

'Meeting's at seven tomorrow night, but be careful lad. He's a dangerous one that Overton.'

***

The following evening Tom was well hidden behind a vast block of Portland stone recently levered from the hillside. He had scouted the area earlier in the day and picked his position with care. Despite the light from the half moon which occasionally flitted out from behind the clouds, he was well hidden. No one could enter the quarry, he thought, without passing his little den. He was well wrapped up against the cold and prepared to wait all night if necessary even if Jed's information turned out to be worthless. Shortly before seven he heard footsteps cautiously making their way down the path into the body of the quarry. The man, carrying a lantern, passed close enough for Tom to recognise Overton. The lieutenant made a cursory search round the flat ground, and then sat down to wait. It was fifteen minutes before anything happened. Tom heard nothing, but suddenly noticed a second figure standing behind Overton. The lieutenant started as he became aware of this presence and leapt to his feet holding the lantern high to identify who it was. The man pushed the light away but not before Tom had recognises the black beard and long greasy ponytail of Nathan Raditch, landlord of the Black Dog.

The two talked urgently together for a few minutes though Tom was too far away to make out the words. Raditch then handed over a small bag and slipped away as silently as he had come. Tom did not doubt that the landlord had been buying favours from Overton, either information or a promise to turn a blind eye, but he realised he had little enough evidence with which to charge a senior officer. Overton's greed was his undoing. Instead of quietly going back to Portland Castle, he could not resist the temptation to check his profit. He placed his lantern on a flat rock and tipped out the contents of the little bag beside it.

It would have been better if Tom had arranged for another witness to be present, or at least had a plan of some sort, but he was determined not to let this chance slip by. 'Good evening Lieutenant.' He crossed the short distance to stand next to Overton who was franticly trying to scrape the pile of guineas back into the bag.

'What are you doing here Vermin?' Overton snarled.

'Perhaps more important, what are you doing Lieutenant, accepting money from Mr Raditch?'

The landlord's name obviously rocked Overton but he quickly returned to the offensive. 'I'm doing the King's business, and there is nothing you can say to prove otherwise.'

'Mr Nathan Raditch will soon be picked up by the militia waiting for him at Smallmouth. He will certainly turn King's evidence to save his own hide, and nothing will give me greater pleasure than to tell the magistrates what I have seen tonight.' Tom was bluffing, but hoped that Overton would not realise this. 'The trial of a revenue officer for taking bribes is just what the new Coast Guard Service needs if corruption is to be stamped out. You're finished Mr Overton.'

'I'll get you, you bastard,' Overton shouted, struggling to pull a pistol from his belt. Before he had time to fire, Tom knocked the lamp from the platform and made a dash for the rocks in the direction he had seen Raditch disappear. The shot when it came passed harmlessly by and Tom scrambled upwards towards the rim of the quarry. He had no plan how to escape. *If Raditch came and went this way, there must be a path somewhere,* he thought. He realised that by coming on his own he had been extremely foolish in challenging Overton. He had left the man with no other option but violence. Tom found a small gap between two huge blocks of limestone. The moon once again slid behind a cloud and he slipped into the narrow passage and waited. *Surely he won't find me here. He must realise searching is useless and go home soon.*

But Overton wasn't going to give up. He relit the lamp and reloaded his pistol and waited for the moon to re-emerge. 'Come on out Verney. We can settle this between us without the need for a fight.' He started to climb the rocks waiting for Tom to appear. 'I know you're short of cash. You can have half the money, if you like.' He started to cast around like a hound seeking a scent, to the left then right, then advancing a few more paces. Tom could hear his footsteps coming closer. He knew that a few yards behind him were the cliffs of the West Weare. These

139

dropped steeply to the sea and were nearly impossible to climb even in daylight. There was no escape for him that way. He wriggled further into his hiding place until he reached the end of the short passage. 'Don't think you can hide from me for ever you little bastard.' Overton's tone changed to a viciousness that left Tom in no doubt what would happen if he were captured. He caught a flash from the lantern as Overton approached the entrance of his hiding place. *If he comes down here I'm finished,* Tom thought. *My only hope is to go upwards.* Cautiously he stood and began to feel the smooth slabs for possible hand holds. There were none. By pressing his back against one slab and forcing his knees against the opposite side he managed to raise himself off the ground. *Like the chimney sweep boys in the big houses,* he thought.

He shuffled upwards again but Overton was listening out for any noise and heard the faint scrabbling sound. 'The rat's trapped in his hole,' he muttered. 'I'll get you now Vermin.' There was a crash as he fired his pistol through the entrance. Tom had no idea where the ball went, but he used the noise to scramble higher until he was able to get his hands over the lip of the slab and lever himself on top. He lay there panting, knowing he wasn't yet safe, but at least he was no longer trapped. He could hear Overton muttering as he reloaded his pistol. Tom peered over the edge and saw the light from the lantern moving slowly down the tunnel. Overton swearing under his breath realised where Tom had gone and went back to try a different approach. Tom felt very exposed as the moon came out from behind a cloud. If the Lieutenant approached from the top of the cliff, he would be able to look down on him and shoot from a distance.

But Overton was determined to kill his victim face to face and almost immediately found another block of stone that leaned at an angle. If he could climb up that, it would lead him to where Tom was lying. With the lantern and pistol in one hand, scaling the slab was a problem but he was driven on by his hatred. Eventually he managed to haul himself almost level with Tom. As his head appeared, Tom kicked out at his face. He felt the nose bone crunch almost at the same moment that the pistol was discharged. Overton fell over backwards and Tom heard the lantern smash followed by a wild scream then silence. Looking over the edge he could see Overton lying on the ground with his right leg trapped between two rocks at an unnatural angle. 'Please help me Verney. My leg's smashed,' Overton whimpered.

Tom scrambled down and stood looking at his enemy now contorted with pain. 'Give me the money,' he said holding out his hand. Overton desperately groped around in his pocket, found what he was looking for and handed the leather bag over to Tom.

'You've busted my nose.' Tom could see that this was true as blood dripped down Overton's chin, but that wasn't the most serious of the lieutenant's problems. He tried to manoeuvre Overton's body so that his broken leg was straighter but this produced a shriek of agony, which convinced Tom there was little he could do on his own. 'Don't leave me,' Overton whimpered, as Tom made ready to go.

'I'd not abandon a dog like this.' Tom turned away. 'I will fetch help, though I doubt if you would have done that for me,' Tom called over his shoulder as he walked into the body of the quarry and from there onto the main track.

One of the drinkers in The Cove House told Tom where the quarry foreman lived and he collected a team to rescue the injured man. Tom reluctantly agreed to show them where he could be found. The quarrymen, quite used to fractures in their rough trade, bound up the broken leg and arranged for him to be taken to Weymouth when Tom reassured them that the Coast Guard Service would pay all fees. Enquiries as to how the accident had happened were met by silence from both Tom and Overton.

Next morning Tom reported to his commanding officer in Weymouth. Bouscarle, perhaps because he was relieved to be rid of Overton even temporarily, chose not to ask searching questions. 'I assume, as second-in-command you would like me to take over from Lieutenant Overton,' Tom said. As this seemed the line of least resistance, Bouscarle readily agreed. 'I would like the appointment to be a permanent one,' Tom added. 'I believe you will not want Lieutenant Overton ever to return when or if he recovers. There are aspects to what happened last night, which will not bring any credit to the service or your command, Sir.' Bouscarle looked confused so Tom produced the leather bag and placed it carefully on the desk. 'I believe I should return this to Nathan Raditch at the Black Dog, as Overton and the Portland Coast Guards will no longer be providing him with the services he believes he has paid for.'

Bouscarle pushed the little bag towards Tom. 'Very well, Verney. I shall recommend that the Board confirm your appointment. Is there anything else you require?' he added a little bitterly.

'Just one more thing sir. I would ask that Hugh Dawkins, currently working out of Poole, be transferred to Portland as Senior Boatman. He is the ideal man to command the *Samphire*.' Tom left the office feeling very pleased with himself. He very much hoped he would never see Saul Overton again.

There was silence when Tom walked into the bar of the Black Dog. He remembered the frightened boy he had been not so long ago on his first visit. Now he was confident in his position. He placed his hat on the bar and waited for attention. The potboy hurried over. 'I would like to speak to Mr Raditch,' Tom said

Eventually the surly landlord emerged from the kitchen. 'What do you want Mr Preventy?'

'I believe this is yours.' He placed the leather bag on the bar pushing it towards Raditch. He was careful to speak loud enough so that everyone in the bar could hear what he said. This was not difficult as all eyes were on him and the silence was total. Even the domino players had suspended their game. 'You should know that Lieutenant Overton is no longer in command of the Portland watch station. Neither I, nor my men will honour whatever you contracted with the lieutenant. Here's your property intact minus only three guineas which I used to pay the quarrymen who took the lieutenant to the infirmary.'

Raditch glowered as he picked up the bag. Tom could see that he had made another enemy, but he had also let all the customers of The Black Dog know exactly what his position was. He then placed a silver sixpence on the bar. 'That is for the meal you gave me when I last visited your pub. The soup was delicious.' He paused and looked slowly round the room. Most of the customers dropped their eyes to concentrate on their drinks. 'Goodbye Mr Raditch, I won't stop for a meal this time.' He picked up his hat and walked out.

Chapter16
The Rescue

Tom kicked the bolster against the door to try and cut down the draught that whistled through the Great Hall of Portland Castle. He threw another log on the fire and watched it blaze into life. The last three months had been a happy time for him. He had decided that as chief officer of the watch station he ought to live in Overton's room in the Master Gunner's Quarters, but he preferred to work in the castle itself. He had left Coast Guard Cottage with regret, but Nat Cropper had asked if he could move in. He explained that it was a Portland tradition that a man couldn't marry until his fiancée became pregnant. With five brothers living together in a small cottage in Chesilton there was little opportunity for that to happen. Tom was happy to give Nat and his Brenda the responsibility of looking after Coast Guard Cottage and the mortar. Perle now took charge of Gussie and this allowed her to visit the castle regularly.

Hugh Dawkins had immediately agreed to join him on Portland and was enjoying himself as captain of the *Samphire*. To Tom's great pleasure Hugh had awkwardly asked his permission to court his sister Amanda and this weekend he was away visiting her in Salisbury. Tom mooched back to the table feeling a little sorry for himself. He had allowed Henry Drake to return to his shop in Wakeham and he had discovered that Matthew, the other Riding Officer on Portland, was not only deaf, but also boring and anti-social. Tom guessed he would be somewhere in the castle, but even if he found him they would have nothing to say to each other. He cursed the gale. Perle wouldn't come over this weekend. The ferry at Smallmouth would not be operating because of the wind and it would be another seven days before he could see her again. He gazed hopelessly at the list of names and figures in the official ledger he was struggling with, feeling lonely and neglected.

He was relieved to be distracted by a knock on the door. The soldier on guard duty showed in a bedraggled Mikey, who stood in front of Tom dripping water onto the carpet. 'Nat told me to come Tom, Sir,' he spluttered. 'There's a ship in the bay as is likely to come aground; not now but in an hour or so. He told me to fetch you and he will gather the lads and move the gun to The Cove.'

Mikey's teeth were chattering so Tom stood him next to the fire to warm up while he collected his waterproof coat and a jacket for the soaking boy. 'Tell Lieutenant Hendrick that he'll need to put a guard on the wreck if she comes ashore,' he told the soldier as he and Mikey hurried out of the castle.

The scene at The Cove House reminded Tom of the hours just before the wreck of the *Arethusa*. Crowds drifted in and out of the snug bar with occasional messages relaying information about the progress of the stricken two-master. This time there was a sense of nervous anticipation from Tom's gun crew huddled together in one corner. They half hoped they would not be needed, but if they were, they had no intention of standing by helplessly as the crew of the doomed vessel drowned. 'She'll come ashore on the Chesil, probably somewhere between Fleet and

Smallmouth,' Sam announced. 'You had best be going.'

Tom was too respectful of the old man's experience to question this and he and Nat Cropper agreed that they should make a start by moving the gun along the top of the pebble bank. Progress was slow as the men slipped and slid along the mile and a half of wet stones with their heavy load, but there were plenty of volunteers to take turns in carrying and a small crowd followed them along the beach. The ship by now was clearly visible a few hundred yards from the surf. She was a two-masted barque, but many of the sails had been blown out to streamers, and by now there was no chance she would be able to claw her way to safety. Tom waited tense, but excited. He guessed that the reputation of the Coast Guard Service in the area might well depend on how successful he was in the next few hours. Fifty yards from the beach the ship struck and lurched drunkenly sideways. One crewmember was catapulted into the surf, and immediately lost to view.

Tom carefully placed the box so that the direction arrow was pointing at the wreck and ordered the wooden sides to be lowered. They had been through their routine day after day even on occasions blindfolded. 'Just like we practised lads,' Tom shouted and he was rewarded by nervous smiles. The gale was at its height as Nat Cropper and Abe Senior pushed and hammered the metal rods into the pebbles until they were firmly fixed. Mikey held onto the modified lobster pot which was in danger of being blown away while Tom and his gun crew prepared the mortar. There was little action from the ship occasionally a crewmember would come on deck and signal something, but then a wave would crash down and the figure would retreat out of sight. In ten minutes the gun was ready to Tom's satisfaction. *Trengrouse's rocket wouldn't work in this wind,* he thought. Nat's line was securely tied to the short chain and the block and tackle were laid out on the ground, as they had been in practice, to ensure that ropes would not get knotted or twisted in flight. 'We've one shot at this,' Tom yelled. 'Are you all ready?'

'We're ready Tom,' Nat answered, and Ted White handed him the glowing match.

The explosion when it came did not disappoint the waiting crowd. The cannon ball sailed skywards dragging the snaking line behind it. It seemed to hover over the masts for a moment and then plunged down to be swallowed by the waves of the far side of the ship. The crowd cheered and clapped. The line was clearly visible lying across the deck. Two crewmembers quickly appeared from a hatchway and started to pull across the heavier rope. Nat and Abe fed out the block and tackle which crept over the waves until, cheered on by the enthusiastic crowd on the beach, it was hauled over the side.

'They're going to make it fast to the base of the mast,' Nat shouted to Tom. 'Tell them it must be tied off higher up.'

Tom waved across to the ship and received an answering wave, but still the rope bowed towards the sea's boiling surface. 'If we send over the lobster pot like that they will all be drowned before they reach safety.' He waved again desperately trying to show the crew that the rope should be secured higher up the mast. His signal was acknowledged, but then nothing happened. Those on board appeared to be waiting for some action from the shore.

'Let me go across and sort them out,' Nat said. 'If I'm over there, I can explain what's needed and with the line clear of the waves they won't even get their feet damp.'

Tom could see the sense in Nat's suggestion, but the journey across would be extremely wet and dangerous. As the only coastguard officer present, he couldn't send one of his volunteers if he was too scared to go himself. 'Good idea Nat, but it has to be me not you. I have the authority when I reach the ship to make them do what we want and I need you here to manage the ropes.' Nat looked as if he was going to protest, but eventually nodded his acceptance. Tom looked at the waves crashing onto the shore. 'Don't try to pull me through the waves. Just hold the line steady when a wave hits and then pull me over when I'm clear.' As an idea it sounded easy enough, but Tom knew he was in for a soaking. Abe organised as many volunteers as he could to man the whip line while Nat hauled it as tight as possible to clear the surf. Mikey helped Tom into the lobster pot, which was then secured to the whip.

Tom was carried down to the shoreline like some sultan on a wickerwork throne. As the next wave crashed onto the pebbles Nat gave the order for the helpers to run with the line up the beach. Tom felt himself jerked out over the sea, and the lobster pot spun round almost tipping him out. His feet were already in the water when a deluge of seawater took him by surprise and found him fighting for breath. *This is what drowning is like*, flashed into his head, but just when he thought his lungs would burst, the cork on the floor of the lobster pot came to his rescue and his head popped clear of the water. Again he found himself rushing out towards the wreck. He was better prepared for the next wave and so were the crew on the beach who held him firm as he submerged then drove him onwards to the side of the ship. Tom was by now exhausted. *I'll not have the energy to climb up*, he thought. *Perhaps I'll just hang here till I drown*. But willing hands were quickly dragging him over the rough planking of the ship's side and he and the lobsterpot flopped onto the deck. Tom was lifted from the basket and bundled down a hatchway. Below deck was a crowd of anxious faces. 'I am the Coast Guard watch captain,' he announced. 'Where's the master?'

'I'm Captain Merriman.' An elderly officer offered a hand to Tom and pulled him to his feet. 'What can you do to help us young man?'

Tom explained the need to secure the tackle higher up the mast to lift the chair clear of the waves and the master understood and immediately instructed two of his sailors to effect this. Below deck the sound of the waves was terrifying and Tom wondered how much longer the dying ship could sustain these hammer blows. Captain Merriman ordered one of his crew to be the first to attempt the crossing. He climbed up the rigging and wriggled into the lobster pot seat. Tom had agreed a system of signals with Nat and as soon as he waved his arms the pot was whisked away high above the waves and quickly landed on the beach. In no time the men pulling on the ropes reversed direction and back came the lobster pot. There were three women on board and Captain Merriman decided that they should be next. Tom directed them to climb the short distance up the mast where a crewmember helped them into the hanging basket. Tom stood on the deck and as soon as each was securely seated and holding on tight he waved across to Nat and the rescue was repeated.

Another wave dashed into the side of the doomed vessel bringing the fore-mast down with a shuddering crash. Even with his limited experience of the sea Tom knew that the end was near. There were twelve crew altogether. Captain Merriman was insistent that he would be the last to leave his ship and when it was only Tom and he left on board, it was the captain who helped Tom into his hanging, floating chair for a second trip and it was he who signalled to the shore crew. This trip was both swifter and safer. Tom quickly found himself lying on the pebbles then helped to his feet by the cheering crowd. He turned to look back at the ship desperate that everyone should be saved. It worried him that the captain might not have the strength to climb into the chair by himself. He need not have been concerned. Captain Merriman was whisked ashore and safely landed next to him. When he managed to clamber to his feet, he searched out Tom and wrung his hand. 'Thank you, young man for all our lives.' Tom introduced the captain to the members of his gun crew and he shook each hand in turn.

'These men are all volunteers,' Tom explained.

'When the owners hear about this, if I still have any standing in the company, I will make sure they are suitably rewarded,' the captain promised.

'What do we do about the ropes, Tom?' Nat asked.

By now Tom was too weary to think coherently. 'Save what you can and get some helpers to bring the gun back to The Cove,' he mumbled. Most of the onlookers were drifting back towards the village and Tom stumbled after them. It seemed a long way away.

Someone grabbed his hand and held on tightly. Looking down he saw that it was Perle. Her soaking dress suggested that she had waded across the lagoon from the cottage in Butter Street. 'Don't you do that again Tom Verney,' she said fiercely. 'I couldn't bear it if you were drowned.' He looked down at her little face so pale and tense with strain.

'It shouldn't happen again,' he said gently, putting a damp arm round her shoulder. 'If there is a next time I will send instructions over with the rope.' Together they walked back to the warmth of The Cove House Inn.

Chapter 17
Planning a Surprise Party

Tom looked round the dilapidated officers' mess in the old Radipole Barracks. 'What are we doing here?' Hugh whispered to him. The two had been summoned to report first to Captain Bouscarle's office and then directed on here by Arthur.

'Why are you whispering? There's no one here.' Tom wandered over to the fireplace to look at the vast oil painting, which dominated the room. A rip in one corner spoiled the picture, but he could make out a fat officer on horseback, with hand raised, standing surrounded by red-coated infantrymen. He read the title: *General Friedrich Wilhelm von Lossberg and his Hessians hold Turkey Hill against the Rebels 28th August 1778.* Tom's father had often told him stories of the American War. From what he could remember this battle must have been one of the few successes of this undistinguished but brutal German regiment. There was other evidence of the barracks' last occupants, the late king's Hessian soldiers; a torn mess book with entries in what Tom guessed was German and some graffiti on one of the walls. The room smelled of decay.

'Someone's coming,' Hugh whispered and Lieutenant Hendrick of the Militia entered. Although Tom and he had both shared accommodation in the Master Gunner's Quarters for some time, they had little to do with each other. The morose lieutenant had his own circle of friends and rejected all Tom's overtures. In the last six months the two had barely spoken. He nodded to Tom and Hugh.

A few minutes later Captain Bouscarle arrived accompanied by the ingratiating Arthur. 'Thank you for coming, gentlemen. I apologise for the mystery, but you will understand why, when I tell you what is planned. Please sit down.' Tom and Hugh found some chairs thrown roughly in a corner and placed them round the table. 'There is one other coming to our meeting and I don't want to start until he is here.' He waited nervously fiddling with some papers he was carrying. The little group sat in silence. There was a noise from outside and Arthur went to the door to let in the last of their party. He was a stout, elderly gentleman dressed in a beige frock coat. A tightly curled white wig capped a florid face and sour expression.

Captain Bouscarle, looking flustered, leaped to his feet. 'Welcome Sir.' He turned to the others. 'Gentlemen, this is Lieutenant Colonel James Frampton of the Queen's Own Dorset Yeomanry. He has agreed to help us in the enterprise I shall outline to you.'

'Let me tell 'em Bouscarle,' Frampton interrupted. 'After all it is my patch of coastline we are talking about. This meeting is supposed to be secret so that the smuggling bastards don't know what we are up to. It appears we have a chance to deal with these Owlers once and for all. Now what's this information you have Bouscarle?'

'There is to be a landing tomorrow night to the east of here and we hear it's likely to be a large one. I can't tell you the exact location but it will be either

Ringstead Bay or Osmington Mills, a stretch of some three miles. We know the signals they will use and the French ship will probably come in either at low tide, which tomorrow will be seven o'clock, or six hours later at high water. Now we are no longer leaking information from our side, there is no reason why we can't surprise them with an ambush and capture the lot.'

'Whatever scum we capture, I will send down for a long time.' Squire Frampton was proud of his reputation as a draconian punisher of miscreants. As a magistrate at Bere Regis or in the Assizes in Dorchester, poor and underprivileged defendants were rarely shown any sympathy from him. 'How reliable is your information?'

Bouscarle looked across at Arthur. 'I have a source who is in the confidence of some of the smugglers. Though we don't know the time of the landing, the rest of my information is certain.'

'You told me that last time,' Frampton growled. 'Each time I bring out the cavalry, the enemy seem to have been warned and disappear. You have a traitor in your organisation Bouscarle.'

'We had a leak, but that has been stopped. This information is sound and our plan will not be betrayed.'

Frampton nodded decisively. 'Right then. I will collect 15 or 20 of my Yeomanry at Moreton House tomorrow afternoon. I expect the villains' land party will assemble at The Smugglers' Inn. The landlord is that bastard Carless, and he is the worst of the lot. Hendrick,' he looked over at the lieutenant, 'you can hide your men in the woods next to the beach at

Osmington. You, whoever you are,' he looked at Tom, 'go to the cliff top at White Nothe with two of Hendrick's men. The enemy will be expecting a signal. Give them a good blazing fire to draw 'em in. I'll look after Ringstead with my cavalry. That's the only other choice for a landing. If they choose Osmington I will come over the cliff to help you Hendrick. If it is Ringstead, you do the same to me. You,' he pointed at Hugh, 'bottle 'em up on the beach and make sure they don't escape to the east. I'll swear in some of my neighbours as special constables and see if we can catch the lot.'

'Perhaps not, Colonel,' Bouscarle said diffidently. 'Some of your neighbours are, I think, sympathetic to the smugglers, and we don't want to lose our surprise.'

'You may be right,' Colonel Frampton admitted grudgingly. 'Is that everything? Anybody have any questions for me?' He looked round at the silent group as if daring them to speak. 'You arrange any details with your men, Bouscarle. I'll see you all tomorrow night. Good hunting!' and he swept from the room.

It was as if on leaving he had sucked all the oxygen out behind him. Captain Bouscarle, sat mouth gaping like a beached cod, the others could think of nothing to say that would not sound like impertinence. Eventually Bouscarle shook himself awake and broke the silence. 'He is a very experienced military office, one of the founding fathers responsible for starting the yeomanry in Dorset. I had other plans,' he folded up the papers he was carrying and slipped them into his pocket, 'but I think it would be sensible to follow Colonel Frampton's suggestions.

He rolled out on the table the map he had been carrying, holding it down with his pistol. 'This is Osmington about five miles to the east of us here in Weymouth.' He pointed out the various features as he spoke. 'Here is Ringstead and Colonel Frampton will come over this hill from Moreton House. This here is the cliff of White Nothe where you will be Verney. I'm sorry. I had intended you to be in charge of the beach party, but I am sure Dawkins will do it just as well. The Colonel is quite right about the landing places. There are only two possibilities, but each depends on the tide. Just off shore from Osmington Mill is an underwater reef called Hannah's Ledge. At low water, which tomorrow evening will be about 7.00 o'clock, smugglers often anchor just outside the Ledge and unload their cargo onto the reef before ferrying it ashore. This means that if the French ship comes in from the west at low water, we know the landing will be by The Smugglers' Inn. But my guess is that this will be too early for them. Ringstead beach on the other hand can only be approached from the east because of this reef known as Crooked Ledge.' He pointed to an area of water just off the shoreline. 'The only real anchorage close to the shore is Bran's Hole here, where there is nine feet of water at high tide.' For the first time Tom was impressed to see Bouscarle's competence and knowledge. When it came to matters of the sea he knew what he was talking about and spoke with confidence. 'These reefs are exposed at low water and to be safe a captain would need to know the area. Neither landing place is comfortable in rough weather. In either place the Frenchie will anchor off shore and the crew will row the goods to the beach. We don't want to make our move until all the contraband is safely landed. We are not so worried about the foreign crew. It's the tubmen we want to capture. Lieutenant Hendrick, how many men can you bring tomorrow night?'

'I will have 14 fit men Sir, all equipped with the Brown Bess.'

'I hope there will be no need to use firearms. I suggest you arrange for Dawkins here to bring half of them across to Weymouth in *Samphire*. The remainder send across the ferry in dribs and drabs starting early in the morning, so as not to arouse suspicion. Get them to rendezvous at Bowleaze around five o'clock in case it is a low tide landing. This will give you plenty of time to be hidden in the woods before seven. Verney, you had better take two of Hendrick's men and be responsible for the signal fire as Colonel Frampton suggested. Light the fire as it gets dark. From the cliff top you will also control the exit for the Smugglers' Path.

Tom was intrigued. 'What's the Smugglers' Path, Sir'.

Arthur spoke for the first time. 'There is a steep and dangerous path from the beach up the cliff face at White Nothe. Locals call it The Zigzag. No smuggler would think to carry contraband up it. One slip is almost certain death. But though treacherous at night it is used sometimes as an escape route.'

'It's a full moon tomorrow night. I expect that's why they chose it. By 11.00 o'clock there will be plenty enough light to see by,' Bouscarle continued.

Dawkins, when you have landed the militiamen in Weymouth, you can pick up my Riding Officers as well as Verney and his two men from the customs' quay and sail round to Lulworth Cove. Leave *Samphire* there. Mr Weld, the squire of Lulworth Castle, has given the Coast Guard vessels permission to anchor whenever we need to. Ringstead is about four miles away. You can make the walk along the cliff top in a couple of hours. Your responsibility will be to block any escape along the beach to the east. Arthur, you know the signals. When you see a light from the Frenchies, it's your job to lure them ashore.'

There's more to Arthur than I realised, Tom thought. *I wonder if he is the source the Captain has such confidence in.*

'That is all gentlemen. I shall take out *The Georgia* tomorrow night and hope to pin the French ship to the shore. Make your way back to Portland tonight as inconspicuously as possible. Remember surprise is vital. To get a conviction we must catch the smugglers with contraband on the beach. Make sure you are armed.' He looked over at Tom and Hugh. 'Pistols and swords for you two, but we shouldn't have any trouble, and I would like to avoid casualties if possible.'

Tom decided not to return to Portland that night, but to visit Joby in Fleet. He drew Hugh to one side. 'When you draw your weapons from the castle armoury will you collect a sword and pistol for me too?' He paused thinking how best to phrase his next question. 'What do you think of our fine colonel?'

'I think he's an overbearing bully,' Hugh said with feeling. 'He may be an excellent soldier and brave enough but my guess is he's unpredictable and will usually act before thinking.'

Tom thought of Overton and Frampton, both unpleasant tyrants but with the law on their side. But then it was landowners like Frampton who made parliamentary laws to their own advantage. He compared those two with the generous Sam Ditchburn, Mikey, the Cropper brothers and others in his gun crew, compassionate and cheerful men who risked their lives when others were in danger even if they had never met them before for very little reward. Perhaps these men might live on the outer edge of the law, but he would much prefer them as friends. He wished his father had been there to give him guidance. Though a strict moralist, Pastor Verney had also been a man of compassion. Right and wrong were not always black and white. Tom hoped he would never have to choose between them.

Chapter 18
The Zigzag Path

Tom stood on the cliff top at White Nothe. Out to sea, he had noticed the sails of a two-masted lugger hovering on the outer edge of Weymouth Bay. He felt certain this was the ship he was to lure into a trap. In the fading light he used the telescope Sir Thomas Hardy had given him to pick out the castle and the dark mass of the island of Portland stretching out to the southwest. From his vantage point he had seen Hugh's party hide themselves in the undergrowth of the landslip a few yards up from the beach. There was no sign yet of Colonel Frampton's cavalry and Bran Point hid the possible landing site at Osmington from view. He remembered a picture his father had shown him of the Emperor Napoleon at the Battle of Wagram. Napoleon was on top of a hill, sitting on his horse Marengo and gazing at the battlefield through a telescope. Tom had his telescope and his battlefield. *Unlike Napoleon*, he thought bitterly, *I shall merely be a spectator.*

'Is the fire big enough, Sir?' Two elderly gunners, Privates Bartlett and Whittock, had been collecting dead bracken and gorse for some time and with Tom's help had built a giant bonfire on the cliff edge.

'See if you can find any more pieces of wood and bracken in case we have to keep the blaze going. Make another pile to the side.' The two men scurried off leaving Tom to his resentment.

The sun had finally sunk beneath the waves to the west when Tom ordered the fire to be lit. He was certain the flames and sparks could be seen well out to sea. Now he had to wait to see if the prey would take the bait. The time of low water and a possible landing at Osmington had passed with out any alarm. An hour later, around the time of high tide, the moon rose out to sea and bathed the scene with a ghostly brightness. Tom recognised the French ship drifting in from the west on the gentle breeze. *It is going to be Ringstead after all*, he thought. *Colonel Frampton will be pleased.*

The sails shivered as the lugger came neatly into the wind close to the shore in Bran's Hole. Even from his high vantage point Tom could hear the rattle of the anchor chain. The crew didn't drop the heavy lugsails as he expected, but braided them to the mast. 'That's so as he can get away quick if *Georgia* comes out of Weymouth, Sir.' Private Bartlett had obviously been in this sort of action before and was keen to demonstrate his knowledge to Tom.

A light appeared on the ship as someone brought a lantern on deck. This was covered and exposed three times. Tom guessed this must be the prearranged signal and assumed that Arthur was down on the beach answering. For some minutes nothing happened and then Tom saw a small rowing boat scurrying like a water beetle towards the beach. Through his spyglass he could clearly see the tubs loaded in the stern. The crew jumped ashore and stacked these on the pebbles, before pushing off and returning to their ship. *I wonder how many trips they will manage before Colonel Frampton makes his move,* he thought.

Dark shapes appeared on the beach from the trees and converged on the pile of barrels and greeted the Frenchmen on their second trip. It all seemed very relaxed. *I wonder who the lander is this time. It's probably too far to the east for Isaac from The Lugger in Chickerell. Most likely it will be Nathan Raditch from The Black Dog or the man Carless that Colonel Frampton spoke of.* The little boat approached the beach for the third time and the shore party dragged it into shallow water. As this happened Tom heard the sound of a hunting horn and along the beach from the direction of Osmington, like some mad ride of the Valkyries, came the coal black forms of Colonel Frampton's cavalry. Tom spun round to look where Hugh and his men had been hiding in time to see them scramble onto the beach and advance on the smugglers.

What followed was total confusion. The compact group surrounding the pile of tubs on the pebbles broke into a melee of scuttling figures like an ant's nest stirred with a stick. From his high vantage point Tom saw a musket or pistol flash from the stern of the rowing boat. More jags of flame immediately followed this from the group on the beach. In the almost still night air he caught the faint crackle of gunfire. At least one of the cavalry fell from his horse and the yeomanry, who had been belabouring the smugglers with the flat of their sabres, started to attack more aggressively. One of Hugh's little group fell to the ground and Tom hoped his friend was safe. Instinctively he noticed a subtle change in the wind. At the top of the tide the wind had dropped completely and now started gently to blow from the land. *It's time for the Frenchman to leave,* he thought. Over towards Weymouth he spotted the faint outline of *The Georgia* as she left the mouth of the Wey. *If the Frenchman leaves now Bouscarle will never be able to trap him on the shore. It will become a chase across the channel with little likelihood of any arrests.*

Tom turned his telescope back to the skirmish on the beach. The rowing boat was scurrying back to the ship and some order was beginning to appear from the brawl around the tubs. There was no sign of Hendrick's men arriving, but some of the cavalry had corralled a few of the smugglers while more fortunate characters darted away into the darkness of the undergrowth. Four figures burst through the cordon and started to run along the beach to the east. One was quickly brought to the ground by two of Hugh's men and a cavalryman started after the escapees. Tom could see, almost immediately, that his horse was having difficulty picking its way between the rocks as the beach became narrower and stonier and it was not long before he gave up the futile chase. The three men stopped running but continued to walk purposefully away from the main action.

To the west *The Georgia* was making little progress against the land breeze. There was still no sign of Hendrick's militia. At sea the Frenchman had hauled his rowing boat on board, untied the braids holding the lugsails to the mast and was gliding away towards the southeast and home. On the beach Tom could see that several of the yeomanry had dismounted and were tending the wounded from both sides. The number of smugglers captured was depressingly small. Colonel Frampton's impulsive charge, before the tubmen had an opportunity to remove the contraband from the beach, had effectively ruined the operation. One customs officer detached himself from the group and started to follow the three along the beach. Tom turned his spyglass on him and thought that he recognised Hugh.

'Those three will be ours in 40 minutes.' Totally involved in the action, Tom had forgotten the two soldiers standing next to him.

'What do you mean by that?' he asked.

'At top tide, there's no passage along the beach,' Private Bartlett said. 'Those three will have to come up the White Nothe either by way of the Burning Cliffs or by the Zigzag. With that officer following them they can't just stop and hide in the Undercliff which is what they would like to do.'

'What is the Undercliff?' Tom asked him.

'See that jumble of rocks and bushes? That's made by landslips from these cliffs. It's full of briars and thorns. There are pathways through it though they're difficult to find. That dark patch is called Burning Cliffs where oil has seeped through the shale. Some would prefer that to the Zigzag as a way to the top. It's less dangerous but awful hard work.'

Tom watched, fascinated, as the tiny figures moved slowly along the beach. Both groups picked their way carefully through the rocks in the moonlight and the distance between them changed very little. The three smugglers reached the end of the beach and scrambling up a muddy bank, disappeared from view. Minutes later the lone pursuer arrived at the same place, hesitated, then followed them up the slope and also disappeared.

'Unless they decide to hide, the next time we see 'em in about ten minutes, will be when they come out from the bushes just below Monument Rock there.' Bartlett pointed to a monstrous slab of limestone that stood like a sentinel at the edge of the Undercliff. 'We'll know then which way they're taking.'

Tom noticed that *The Georgia* had turned round and was tacking back to Weymouth. The French lugger was almost out of sight.

'Hendrick's arrived.' Private Whittock pointed down to the beach where the soldiers could be seen taking over responsibility for the prisoners from the cavalry. Each horseman hoisted one of the tubs onto the pommel of his saddle and Tom's first thought was to wonder how many of those would eventually be deposited in the Customs House at Weymouth. He immediately regretted his own cynicism.

'There they are Sir.' Tom saw where Bartlett was pointing as three figures, just visible in the moonlight, emerged from the scrub. They paused by Monument Rock and two turned to the right and one continued on the path to the left. 'Them two is coming up the cliffs, Sir. Arthur and I can look after them if you can manage t'other one.' Tom agreed and the two soldiers hurried off along the cliff top following the line of white stones placed by earlier Riding Officers to mark the path. By now the pursuing customs officer had reached the monument rock. He hesitated a moment before deciding to continue along the chalk path. When the man looked up at the cliff Tom could see clearly that it was Hugh Dawkins. The lone smuggler was now committed to the Zigzag and between them they had him trapped.

Both men climbed carefully aware that there were many places where any slip could be fatal. There were moments when they passed out of Tom's sight, and then as the path doubled back each would come into his view. Hugh was some way behind the smuggler and appeared to be labouring for breath. As the gradient grew steeper there were moments when the two were physically quite close though the smuggler was higher up the cliff face. At one such time Tom heard Hugh call out and saw him draw his pistol. *Please don't*, he thought and started to call out. As he drew breath to shout a warning, he saw Hugh's pistol flash, the smuggler stumble and Hugh slipped and fell over backwards. This was closely followed by the crack of the explosion and then silence. Tom could see no movement. He stood where the path arrived at the cliff top for a moment undecided and then cautiously he started to descend. The moonlight was sufficient for him to pick his way, but the steep track fell away sharply below him and twice he slipped over and had to scramble carefully to his feet again. He soon arrived at the place where he had seen the smuggler fall, but there was no sign of him. *Where has he disappeared to, and where has Hugh gone.* He carried on slipping and sliding down. Round one more bend he heard a voice calling out for help. He peered over the edge and saw two figures one above the other lying against the cliff where it dropped straight down into the sea.

'I can't hold him much longer.' The smuggler had hold of Hugh's arm and had jammed his own body between two rocks to stop them both being dragged over the edge.

Hugh appeared to be unconscious and was certainly incapable of helping himself. 'Hold on,' Tom said in a voice that at least sounded calm. 'I'm coming down.'

'Is that you Tom? I hoped it might be. It's Jacko here.' There was a pause as he shifted his weight to get a stronger hold on Hugh. 'I've taken a shot to the shoulder. I don't think anything is broken, but I've already lost a fair amount of blood and am weakening. You'd better get down here fast.'

Tom edged his way down until he was lying next to Jacko and found a small boulder to brace his feet against. The three of them were lying in a perilous position with one unconscious and one wounded. Hugh groaned.

'What happened to him?' Tom asked.

'He must have slipped when he fired the pistol. Silly bugger forgot to brace himself I expect. Then he bashed his head. I caught him just as he was rolling over the edge.'

'Give me his arm.' Jacko handed over the arm he had been holding. 'You crawl up a bit Jacko and I'll see if I can drag him up to you. The track is only two or three feet above you.' Tom was able to haul Hugh's limp body a short distance, and when Jacko held the arm again he was able to grab Hugh's belt and repeat the movement. Slowly, a few inches at a time, they were able to ease their way upwards until all three of them were lying on the narrow path.

Hugh groaned and his eyes fluttered open. 'Take a drink.' Jacko held a leather bottle to his lips and Hugh swallowed a mouthful of water.

'What happened?' Hugh asked.

'You shot me and fell over backwards,' Jacko told him bluntly.

'This is Jacko, Hugh.' Tom felt it was not the time for more formal introductions. 'He's Perle's brother and has just saved your life.' As the only one uninjured he knew he had to take control. 'It's about five minutes to the top. Jacko's wounded and it's too narrow for me to carry you up. We can give you support, but you're going to have to make most of the effort yourself.' He hauled Hugh to his feet.

As he swayed dizzily Tom pinned him against the cliff face. 'You brace him from the back Jacko, and he can lean on me as we go.' The trio shuffled forward and painfully slowly began to climb. At the first elbow, the path was too narrow and steep for Tom to support Hugh's sagging body. The three of them dropped to their knees and successfully crawled round the bend. They repeated this on the next corner. There were no more particular adventures but it was more fifteen minutes than five before they reached the top. Jacko immediately sat down heavily, holding his shoulder. 'I can't go on at the moment Tom,' he said. 'I'll be all right in a little while but I need to rest.' He lay back on the grass and closed his eyes. Hugh, still shocked by his narrow escape, sat down next to him.

It was a fine evening and not too cold. Each of them would have been happy to rest there for some time, but Tom heard the militia soldiers returning along the cliff top. He was galvanised into action. 'Hugh, get to your feet and try to appear as natural as you can. First help me drag Jacko over to the fire. You must lie quiet,' he told him. 'I cannot have the soldiers knowing you are here.' He completely covered the boy with the dried bracken collected for the bonfire. It was scanty cover but would have to do.

'No luck with us, Sir. The two men must have slipped past us,' Private Bartlett seemed anxious to excuse their lack of success. 'We had to go right down the hill to try and cut them off, but when we looked for them they had disappeared. Either we missed them or they are still hiding in the briars. Isn't that right Arthur?'

Arthur Whittock looked down at his boots and muttered a half hearted 'Aye.'

Tom guessed they had encountered the two smugglers and recognising them, had let them go. Still, he couldn't blame them as he was going to do much the same himself. 'By the time Mr Dawkins arrived at the top our man had given us the slip.' He realised that the men might well have heard Hugh's pistol fire so he quickly invented a situation where Hugh had fired at a fleeing shadowy figure. The story sounded feeble enough to him, but whether the men believed it or not they were in no position to challenge an officer. He ordered them to return to Lieutenant Hendrick and help escort the prisoners back to Weymouth.

'Shall I build up the fire before we go?' Bartlett asked moving forward.

Tom placed himself between the man and the hidden Jacko. 'I gave you an order soldier,' he said icily. 'Do it immediately.'

Neither of them said anything for some minutes as the sound of footfalls faded along the cliff. Then Tom moved forward to remove the dead bracken from Jacko. The boy did not look well but did manage a feeble grin. 'What do we do now Tom?' Hugh asked anxiously.

Only twenty-four hours earlier Tom had been concerned how he would resolve his moral dilemma, working as a King's officer with friends who might well be smugglers. When it came to the moment of decision there was no problem. 'Jacko once saved my life and has just saved yours too Hugh. I'm going to marry his sister. I refuse to hand him over to that brute Frampton. If one of the yeomanry on the beach is dead this night's work could result in a hanging. At best it will mean transportation to Australia. I'll not have that for Jacko.'

'Does that mean you're going to marry Perle?' Jacko asked. He seemed remarkably unperturbed about the dangers of his position.

'Unless you have another sister I don't know about, I suppose it does.' Tom was surprised how comfortable he felt with that idea. 'First we must move you to safety and get your wound treated.' He peeled back Jacko's jacket and shirt to see what sort of a mess Hugh's bullet had made. The wound was no longer bleeding, but the ugly gash just below his shoulder blade was obviously causing him pain and he had lost a quantity of blood. Hugh was still shaking from the blow to his head and joined Jacko on the grass. While Tom made up the fire to keep them both warm they made a plan of action.

'What happened down there?' Tom asked.

'That idiot Frampton charged in with his yeomanry before all the contraband had been landed,' Hugh answered. 'Someone opened fire and then it was mayhem.'

'It was one of the Frenchmen who panicked,' Jacko interrupted. 'We suddenly saw these black figures rushing towards us. Several of the crew of Le Pegasus d'Argent, that was the boat that brought me over, had pistols though they had been told by the captain to leave them on board. They lost their nerve when they saw the horses and the result was the chaos you saw.' There was a long pause while the three of them looked back on the brawl on the beach. 'I didn't come as a smuggler. I hitched a lift as I wanted to see Ma and Perle.' He fished in his jacket pocket and brought out a second leather bottle. 'Both of you look as if you could do with a drink.'

This is probably not the first occasion I have drunk smuggled brandy, Tom thought, *but it can't be too often that a customs officer drinks with a smuggler at the site of a landing.*

Jacko was obviously now in considerable pain and suffering from shock. 'If you can set me on the way to Ma's cottage,' he said, 'I'd better be going or all of us will be in trouble.'

'You'll never make it by yourself,' Hugh answered. 'You're already too weak and Colonel Frampton and his thugs are bound to be searching for stragglers. They'll quickly pick you up. As Tom said, necks will be stretched for what happened here, and I won't have that for you.'

'We will take you back with us to the castle,' Tom said. Even if the magistrates hear that you landed from the *Pegasus*, they will never think to look for you in an army barracks. *The Samphire* is in Lulworth Cove. It will take some time but Hugh and I can help you reach there and then we'll sail back to Portland with you. When you have recovered you can make your own way back to France.

Despite Jacko's protests Hugh and Tom, thought the plan would work and together they began carrying him along the cliff path away from the scene of their misadventure.

Chapter 19
Donkey's Ear and Maggots

'Send for Perle; she'll know what to do,' Jacko said weakly. It was four days since Hugh and Tom had carried a barely conscious Jacko into the Master Gunner's Quarters and hidden him in Tom's bedroom. Surprisingly there had been no problems concealing him. Lieutenant Hendrick was spending the night in Weymouth and Matthew, the only other member of the Coastguard Service resident in the castle, showed no interest in their activities.   Tom wiped Jacko's face with a damp cloth.   He was desperately worried about his friend and had no idea what to do next. Jacko was obviously running a temperature. The area around the wound was festering and livid streaks of red were becoming visible under his arm. Tom dared not summon a doctor, as he was sure that the authorities would quickly learn of Jacko's presence. He had little concern for his own compromised position, but Frampton, acting as the local magistrate, had already sentenced three of the local smugglers to transportation and they would soon be on their way to Van Diemen's Land. One of the French crew caught with a pistol was waiting trial at the Assizes for murder. He would not let this happen to Jacko.

'Why Perle?' he asked. 'What can she do?'

Jacko smiled faintly. 'You'll see. Perle has more common sense than all three of us put together. She'll know what to do.'

Tom asked Mikey to fetch Perle. 'Tell her it is important she comes immediately,' he told the unsuspecting boy. When she arrived next afternoon on Gussie, Tom was concerned that she should not be too shocked by Jacko's appearance. He need not have worried.

'Oh, Jacko. What ever have you been up to?' she addressed her barely conscious brother. As she was speaking she removed the rough bandaging Tom had placed over the wound and sniffed at it, wrinkling her nose in distaste. 'Help me sit him up,' she ordered and quickly established that the musket ball had left no exit wound. 'It's still in there.' She gently laid him back on the bed. 'I take it he can't see a doctor, so you will have to take it out,' she said looking at Tom. 'If you don't, he will die. He has already been like this too long. Look, the flesh around the wound is already decaying. He also has blood poisoning.'

'How do you know all this?' Hugh asked.

'I've helped Isaac with enough wounds,' she shrugged. 'Guess I just picked it up. I would get Isaac to come and deal with it, but there is no chance he will enter this castle. I know he will lend me cloths for bandages, pincers and a knife and I will bring those with me tomorrow early. He will tell me what else I should bring. There's a lot to do, so I will go now, but I'll be back early tomorrow morning.' She kissed Jacko briefly on the forehead. 'Clean up the wound as best you can and make him comfortable,' she told Tom over her shoulder as she left the room. 'Makes sure he has some brandy left. Tomorrow will be difficult for him.'

Tom and Hugh looked at each other, shocked by her decisiveness. 'Who's Isaac?' Hugh asked.

'He's the landlord of The Lugger Inn,' Tom answered.

'And he once nearly killed Tom,' Jacko croaked. 'Don't worry about Perle. I told you she would know what to do,' his voice little more than a whisper. 'She's as good as any doctor.'

***

Perle returned to the Castle soon after dawn. 'There's an old man snooping around outside the window,' she reported. 'I don't like it. Please get rid of him Tom.'

'That'll be Matthew,' Tom said, hurrying off. He returned ten minutes later to let the others know that Matthew was now on an expedition to Portland Bill to see if there was any smuggling activity on the east coast of the island.

Perle had already unfolded a towel on the table next to Jacko's bed and laid on it a vicious looking knife and some large pincers. Next to these were two jars one was filled with leaves and the other seemed to be filled with live bait.

'Are you going fishing after?' Jacko asked. A night's rest had helped him to feel slightly better, but he was still flushed and feverish.

Perle looked at him severely. 'I can make a guess what you've been doing Jacko, but I don't want to know. You're my brother and I love you, though you've caused pain to me and ma. Tom must take the bullet out of your shoulder, as the wound is festering. It'll hurt like the devil, but it's the only way. If it doesn't come out you will die.'

'I don't know what to do.' Tom was pale and shaking. 'You seem to know all about it Perle. It's better if you do it.'

'No Tom. Surgeoning has always been man's work. I'm told it's against natural law for a girl to cut into a man.' She stood looking at him till he nodded in agreement. 'Hugh and I will help you and when the cutting's done, I'll show you what to do to help the wound heal.' She picked up the leather flask lying beside the bed. 'Now you can drink as much as you want Jacko. It'll help with the pain.'

As Jacko upended the flask, she handed the knife to Tom and told Hugh to stand on the other side of the bed with a clean cloth. 'When Tom cuts there will be a deal of blood. Your job is to keep the area dry.' She then began to press hard with her fingertips around the wound until Jacko let out a yelp. 'There,' she said to Tom pointing at the spot. 'That's where the ball lies.'

Tom wiped his forehead with the sleeve of his shirt and poked gently at Jacko's skin with the point of the knife. 'Shall I cut away the dead flesh first?' he asked.

'Maggots will look after that later,' Perle said tersely. 'Isaac says to cut firm and cut deep.'

Tom made an incision where Perle had suggested and the flesh opened up like two smiling lips. Hugh mopped up the blood that flowed and Jacko groaned. 'Deeper Tom.' Tom could see that Perle was tense with worry. Now was not the time to hold back. He cut again opening a gash two inches long and Jacko let out a cry as he felt the blade grate against something hard. 'I think I've hit his shoulder blade,' he muttered. 'The bullet must be somewhere else. I don't think I can do this.' He straightened up and started to pull back.

'Feel with your fingers,' Perle urged him on.

Tom bent forward again and pushed his forefinger into the wound. 'There's something here,' he said hooking his finger around and pulling it out. He held up a soggy piece of material. 'That's from Jacko's shirt. The bullet must be right behind it.'

While Hugh cleaned up the blood again Tom picked up the pincers. 'I'll see if I can grab it with these.' He pushed the pincers into the cut he had made in the shoulder and felt them grate against the piece of metal. Jacko cried out again and began to thrash about. 'Hold him still,' Tom shouted at Hugh. 'I can't get it out if he's moving all over the place.' Hugh threw his body over Jacko's other arm and shoulder while Tom discarded the pincers and dived into the wound with thumb and forefinger. He felt the bullet, pinched it tight and tugged it out. Jacko moaned and passed out as Tom triumphantly held up the tiny, misshapen metal sphere.

He wanted to sit down in relief, but Perle wasn't finished. She picked up the jar of live bait and started to sprinkle the skinny, white grubs into the wound. From her apron pocket she took out a large cork, which had started life as the stopper on a wine cask. This had been hollowed out and holes had been pricked all over the top to form a little pouch. 'They're fly maggots,' she explained to the startled boys. 'We must keep them in this cage over the wound for two days. The holes are so the maggots can breath. I expect them to eat all the dead flesh and leave the wound clean. When that's done we can draw the poison from his blood. Now help me tie the cork in place.' The three of them worked together to bind up Jacko's shoulder with its strange, caged menagerie in place. 'You two go and clean up,' Perle suggested when they had finished. 'I'll sit with Jacko till he wakes up.

***

Two days later Perle returned to the castle again carrying her two glass jars. Jacko was awake, but still sweating and feverish. The glands in his armpit and groin were swollen and throbbing. Perle carefully removed the bandaging from his shoulder and looked with pleasure at the fat, slug-like maggots, which were contained in the cork. She sniffed at the wound, which now looked pink and clean. 'Maggots have eaten their fill,' she said. 'I'll take them back to Goody Conway,' and she tipped them into the first jar. From the second she tipped out a mass of dried leaves. This is hedge woundwort. Folks around here call it Donkey's Ear. If we bind this over the infected area, Goody Conway says it will draw the poison from his blood.'

The problem of what to do with Jacko remained. Five days after Tom had removed the bullet he was still weak and the bandages, which were changed daily, were invariably stained with an evil-smelling pus. 'Though you have almost certainly saved his life,' Hugh said, 'he still needs to see a doctor as the Donkey's Ear stuff isn't doing what it should.'

It was Jacko himself who came up with the answer. 'You two can manage *Samphire*. Take me

179

over to Alderney. It's the most northerly of the Channel Islands. Though it's a crown dependency, the governor, he's called Henri Le Mesurier, likes smugglers and is happy for them to use it as a base. We sailed from there in the *Silver Pegasus* and I will be quite safe in La Ville where I know lots of people. *Samphire* can manage the trip easily.'

Hugh was excited by the idea, but Tom had reservations. 'Isn't *Samphire* too small to journey across the channel?

Jacko and Hugh both laughed at his caution and persuaded him that it would be fun. It was agreed that Tom should tell Captain Bouscarle that they intended to go to the Channel Islands to investigate the smuggling there. 'The journey will take from 10 to 12 hours if the wind is helpful,' Jacko told them. 'We should wait for a westerly. If the wind blows from the southwest we would have to beat across and that will take too long. I guess it must be about 56 miles from here.' He sat up in bed excited by the prospect of a sea journey. 'The harbour on Alderney is at Braye on the north of the island. It has a tricky, rocky entrance and we must be careful of the powerful tide race. I wouldn't like to try it after dark. We could set off at 4.00 or 5.00 in the morning and this would leave us plenty of time to arrive in the light.'

When Perle heard the plan she told them that she too would be on board. 'Jacko still needs someone to nurse him and I can do that. I have told Ma that you are here Jacko but though she wanted to come and visit you, I told her 'No.' It'd be too dangerous for you. She will make up a hamper of food for us and I know she has a little money hidden away, which she will let us have.'

They agreed that the plan should be put into effect as soon as possible and each of them went off to make the necessary preparations.

Chapter 20
A Sailing Trip

As the sun rose out of the sea to the east, the little cutter surged through the waves making five or six knots on the steady westerly wind. *Samphire* had crossed The Shambles sandbar off Portland Bill in the dark. Hugh was steering due south on a course he had worked out the previous evening and they were already well into the English Channel. Tom had been nervous about his ability to help Hugh on his own for the return trip from Alderney and had decided to ask Nat Cropper to come with them. Besides having the reputation as one of the finest sailors on Portland, Nat was now settled into Coast Guard Cottage and Tom reckoned he was responsible enough to be entrusted with their secret. He greeted Jacko cheerfully and chose not to ask why they were leaving while it was still dark with a wounded young man on board.

There had been one tense moment as Hugh and Tom carried Jacko on board. One of the 'extramen', who Hugh sometimes used as an additional crew member, had staggered out of the Mermaid pub and offered his services for whatever journey *Samphire* was about to make. Hugh had spun him some complicated story and the happy drunk had returned to the pub apparently satisfied.

Perle, who was not an enthusiastic sailor, stayed below in the tiny half-cabin while Tom and Nat handled the sails and Hugh steered. Joby de Bretton had provided a hamper of food and a lunch of meat pie and cheese washed down with a rough (probably smuggled) red wine put them all in a cheerful mood.

Tom's main concern was for Jacko's health. Hugh and Nat seemed confident enough in handling *Samphire,* but Jacko was the only member of the party who had actually been to Alderney and he was running a fever and frequently lapsing into sleep or unconsciousness. He had warned Hugh that coming into Braye harbour was not easy, particularly if there was a strong tide running. Hugh needed Jacko on deck to show them the marker posts if they were to hit off the difficult entrance.

As the afternoon progressed the wind freshened and Hugh discussed with Nat the wisdom of reefing the sail. Both were anxious to arrive at Alderney while it was still light and *Samphire* seemed to be handling the conditions well. Around 4.00 o'clock the island appeared as a black smudge on the horizon and Hugh pleased with his navigation altered course a couple of points. They would arrive at the north end of the island with plenty of light left. Tom went down to see how Jacko was faring and Perle told him that he had fallen asleep 15 minutes earlier. He decided not to disturb him yet.

The wind was edging round to the southwest and whipping spray off the tops of the waves as they raced in the final miles. Hugh anxiously asked Tom if Jacko was now awake. He had decided to come into Braye harbour leaving the little island of Burhou well to his starboard, but now he was getting nervous about the rocks on the northern point of Alderney and the strong tidal flow. Tom told him that Jacko was not fit to come on deck but passed on the message that if he lined a red and white marker post with the spire of St Anne's church he should see the entrance clearly. Perhaps rather belatedly Hugh and Nat decided to put a reef in the sail and while the little boat was hove to they found themselves inexorably dragged eastwards by the tidal surge. Wind and tide were now pushing in the same direction and it quickly became obvious that *Samphire* was not going to make Braye harbour on this tack. Hugh tried going about, but the tide was too strong for them to push the bows through the wind.

'We're not going to make the harbour,' Hugh shouted to Nat as the strength of the wind increased. He pushed the tiller over and the little boat spun to the north relieved to be no longer battling against the elements. 'We will have to go round the eastern point of Alderney. That means going through the Race. Tell them to hang on below. It's going to get rough.' Ahead of them Tom could see a maelstrom of churning water and he just had time to remember Homer's description of the whirlpool Charybdis, which Odysseus tried to avoid as he returned to Ithica. At least ten knots of tide and a strong south-westerly drove *Samphire* forward into the chaos. Water poured over the bows and on two occasions as the boat slewed sideways in the conflict of waves, he felt certain they were lost.

An anxious Perle poked her head out of the cabin. How much longer is this going to last?' she asked. 'Jacko is being thrown all over down here.'

Suddenly they were through the worst and racing towards the Normandy coast. 'We will have to beach up tonight Tom,' Hugh shouted to him through cupped hands. 'There are plenty of isolated coves to choose from.'

'Coast Guards are not supposed to land in France,' Tom shouted back. 'But we have already broken so many rules one more won't make any difference.' They grinned at each other in excitement and relief.

Hugh identified a sandy bay, which they later found was called Goury and dropping the sails, with wind and tide behind them, ran *Samphire* onto the beach. Perle, confident in her French language went ashore to find out where they were, and returned half an hour later to say that Goury had a tiny inn or auberge where their limited funds would run to providing Jacko with a bed for the night. There was also a doctor in the next village of Auderville and the innkeeper told her for a few more silver pennies he might be persuaded to come out to see the injured boy. Hugh bedded the boat down for the night while Nat and Tom carried Jacko to the auberge and made him as comfortable as possible. Tom then set off to walk the five miles to Auderville to see if he could persuade the doctor to come back to Goury that evening.

***

The return trip to Portland lacked the excitement of the outward voyage. The doctor from Auderville had cleaned and drained some fluid from Jacko's shoulder. A mixture of bitter herbs had reduced the infection and next morning on a gentle breeze and ebbing tide the short journey from the Normandy coast to Alderney had been simple. Perle had found an ideal room for herself and Jacko above the baker's shop though to Perle's suspicious mind the baker's daughter Suzanna seemed unnecessarily delighted to see Jacko again. Tom and Hugh gave Perle all the money they had and she promised to return to Dorset as soon as Jacko was fully fit. Before *Samphire* left Braye harbour next morning Perle drew Tom aside. 'Jacko tells me that you would like us to be wed.' She paused, and Tom could think of nothing appropriate to say. With the drama of the following days he had quite forgotten the casual remark he had made on the top of White Nothe, 'I think perhaps you should have asked me before you thought to tell my brother.' She looked at him seriously but he could sense that she was enjoying his confusion.

'Come on Tom,' Hugh shouted across the jetty. 'We must leave straight away if we want to catch the tide.'

'Do you want to marry me?' Tom blurted out.

'I'll think about it,' Perle smiled at him. 'I'll tell you when I'm back in Dorset.

Though the wind was contrary and the return journey took considerably longer than their helter-skelter trip to the Normandy coast, they had few problems and Nat was confident about landing on Portland in the dark. No one there seemed concerned about their absence or their return.

Next morning Tom went to see a much relieved Joby to tell her the news about Jacko and Perle and called in at the Customs House. He thought it would be tactful to make some sort of a report to Captain Bouscarle about his trip, but he found his superior listless and unwell. He showed little interest about where *Samphire* had been and a much-relieved Tom quickly returned to Portland. Later, in the snug of The Cove House Inn Sam Ditchburn asked him if he had enjoyed his trip in *Samphire*. Tom was not certain if there was a secret twinkle in the old man's eye as he asked, but when Tom declined to give any information he seemed happy to let the matter drop.

Chapter 21
Prospects

During the next weeks Tom was kept busy setting up daily routines for his watch station. He had asked Nat Cropper to take over command of the mortar crew, promising him that there would be a small financial reward every time the team was called out. Later he was to learn that this was the first civilian lifesaving team in the country, a practice that was widely copied when the Portland experiment was shown to be so successful.

Five weeks after the expedition to Alderney, Joby de Breton received a message from Perle via a stranger who came to the bar at the Lugger Inn asking for her. She brought Gussie over to the Castle to pass on to Tom the news that Jacko was making an excellent recovery and seemed none the worse for his accident. Perle said she was missing him. It seemed an ideal moment for Tom to tell Joby that he wanted to marry her daughter. Joby laughed. 'She told me that would happen many months ago.'

Towards the end of December, Captain Bouscarle sent for him. Tom had never really liked his inadequate superior, but he was dismayed to see how gaunt and sickly he now looked. 'Sit down Tom and thank you for coming. I have been impressed with what you have achieved in Portland.' He pressed a handkerchief to his lips to stifle a bout of coughing. 'You can see that I am not well. I intend to resign my post.' He took a sip of water and Tom could not fail to notice that his hand was shaking badly. 'I would like you to take over from me here, but of course it is not my appointment to make.' He paused and Tom wondered if he should say something, but Bouscarle carried on. 'We need to exercise a certain amount of cunning with the Board or they will appoint someone totally unsuitable for Dorset to take my place. I have not yet told either your godfather in Poole or the Board in London that I intend to resign. I want you to put your affairs in order over at the castle. Young Dawkins can take your place temporarily and, who knows, the Board may even make his appointment permanent. You will come and work with me here. Arthur and I will teach you everything you need to know about my job. As Collector here in Weymouth you must not only try to prevent smuggling, but you would also be responsible for the collection of import duties and all the statistics the government requires about exports and shipping. In addition our office is responsible for wrecks, and should the government so require the press gang and protection of the coastline.'

The effort of talking exhausted Bouscarle, and Tom thought it might be useful if he broke into the conversation. 'There seems much more to the job than I had realised. How long do you think I will need to learn all those things?'

'I will be resigning in one month's time. I have been watching your progress Tom and I think you have a bright future in The Service. You are clever and honest, qualities that are not present in many officers. Also people trust you.'

This praise from the normally taciturn Bouscarle embarrassed Tom. He was aware that he had not always been honest with him nor trustworthy. He squirmed uncomfortably. 'I ought to tell you that there have been occasions when I have not been entirely straight with you Sir.'

Bouscarle smiled and waved his hand dismissively. 'If you mean that business with Jacques de Bretton on the night of the Ringstead landing, I think you did the right thing. If you had asked me about it, I would have had to say 'no'. But should that idiot Frampton have laid his hands on Jacques it would have set back the service here in Weymouth for years.'

'How did you know?' Tom asked.

'Don't expect me to give away all my secrets.' Bouscarle signalled Tom to leave. 'Go and make the necessary arrangements at the castle. You start here tomorrow.' As Tom reached the door, Bouscarle called him back. 'Tomorrow night there is to be a landing on Chesil, opposite Fleet village. It's not a smuggling operation so there is no need to have officers there, but I suggest you go to meet the boat just after moonrise. Don't wear your uniform or you might scare the captain away.' He picked up his pen and started to write in the ledger on the desk.

Tom waited anxiously as the rowing boat skimmed over the water and ran aground on the beach. A single cloaked figure climbed out over the bows then helped push the boat out again into the surf. It was Perle who started to walk up the steep shingle bank. Tom knew by her limp that she was tired. He hurried down to greet her. 'I hope you'd be here,' she said wearily as he wrapped her in his arms. Tom levered her away and held her at arms length. 'Perle de Bretton, will you marry me?'

'Of course I will you mutt,' she said, and forced herself back into his embrace.

Chapter 22
A Wedding

Jim Bouscarle's assessment of the Board's position proved to be accurate. Tom was appointed as temporary Comptroller of Customs at Weymouth. His uncle, Toby Fortescue, pointed out in a letter of congratulations that Tom was the youngest in the country to hold this position, but in a nation that had recently accepted William Pitt as chancellor of the exchequer aged 23 and prime minister at 25 there was no barrier to youth holding positions of responsibility.

One month after Perle had returned from the Alderney, Hugh had nervously come to ask Tom if he would consent to his marrying his elder sister Amanda. A delighted Tom was happy to agree, but his mind was now firmly fixed on his own wedding. A date was fixed in early summer and a letter was sent to Jacko telling him that he was required to give away his sister. Hugh had agreed to be the best man. Joby began the preparations for the wedding party. Lady Hardy had suggested that Portesham House might be suitable for the reception, but in the end a generous offer from Major and Mrs Wallace to host the affair in Waddon House, two miles outside Portesham, was gladly accepted. Tom hoped for a relatively small affair, but this had not taken into account the importance of his new position and the local popularity of the de Bretton family.

The wedding itself in St Peter's Portesham was simple and brief. Despite being forced into formal clothes, Jacko, with a red bandana and his hair tied back in a ponytail, still managed to look like a pirate as he escorted his sister up the aisle. The piratical effect was increased by his broad wink to the Hardy daughters as he passed them.

Two hours later Tom stood by the fireplace in the grand saloon of Waddon House watching his guests enjoy themselves. His godfather, Toby Fortescue, was the only person determined not to join in the celebrations. He sat morosely on his own in a corner. Mrs Wallace, with Joby's help, had produced an excellent feast. Joby had asked if Isaac from The Lugger Inn could be invited, but Tom, remembering his first day as a Riding Officer and his assault on Chesil Beach, had refused. He noticed his sailing mentor Petty Officer Blake proudly introducing his wife to Sir Thomas Hardy. Lady Anna Hardy was chatting to Sam Ditchburn while at the same time trying to keep her eye on three lively teenage daughters. The gun crew were all present, smartened up by Nat Cropper, though Mikey found it difficult not to gawp at the opulence of the house. Jim Bouscarle, now chair-bound, was chatting to Aunt Edith who had brought Beth and Amanda over from Salisbury for the wedding. While Tom was thinking of his younger sister she came and stood next to him, slipping her hand into his. 'I am sad that papa is not here to enjoy this,' she whispered.

'I think he would have been pleased,' Tom answered.

'And proud of you too.'

Perle, looking pretty and happy came to stand on Tom's other side. She leaned over to Beth. 'Tom and I would be very pleased if you choose to come and live with us in Weymouth. Amanda and Hugh will soon by wed and you might be lonely in Salisbury.'

'I think I would like to stay with Aunt Edith for the time being. She has grown used to having company, and...' Tom noticed a blush steal across her cheeks, 'I would miss my friends.'

It will be a lucky man, thought Tom, *who captures the heart of pretty, lively Beth.*

Tom had not wanted any speeches at the reception, but Admiral Sir Thomas Hardy had requested that he be allowed to say a very few words and Tom had though it would be rude to refuse him. Major Wallace called for quiet, and Dorset's greatest sailor walked to the middle of the room.

'Where's Jacko,' Tom whispered to Perle.

'I saw him slip outside with Louisa ten minutes ago,' she answered calmly. 'I think Lady H suspects something, but I hope the Admiral doesn't notice she's gone.'

The Admiral however was concentrating on his 'few words.' He started by talking about Perle and how she was like another daughter to him. As he did so his eyes glanced round the room, looking for his family, and Lady Hardy smiled at him encouragingly. The Admiral's spoke as if he was addressing his crew during a force eight gale, but such was the respect in which he was held by all present that no one wanted to laugh at his forceful delivery. He sung Tom's praise pointing out how he had early on detected his suitability for responsibility and promotion and predicted an excellent future for him. 'There will come a time shortly when the Free Trade Movement becomes the accepted political creed of this land.

Smuggling will die out, not because of successful action by the Revenue, but because it is no longer profitable. The responsibility of the Coast Guard Service will then be taking charge of wrecks, saving lives and protecting property. As international trade increases, it is young men like Tom, supported by the excellent work of the Portland lifesaving crew, who will help to keep our sailors safe. I ask you to raise your glasses to these two young people and to all who help make Britain great and her people safe.'

Though not everyone present had seen the relevance of Sir Thomas's speech, it was met with enthusiastic cheers. *At least it was short*, Tom thought. He led Perle over to one of the long windows. In the distance they could see a flash of the sea in Lyme Bay bounded by the long curve of the island of Portland where the foundations for so much of his present happiness had been laid. It had not been an easy journey nor a straightforward one, but he did not think has father would have disapproved of the twists and turns he had taken.

EPILOGUE

In 1826, before leading a British squadron on an expedition to Lisbon, Admiral Hardy further recommended Tom Verney's usefulness to the Customs Board. As a result of this Tom was asked to organise trials at Freshwater in the Isle of Wight to help the Royal National Institute for Saving Life from Shipwreck decide whether to favour the Manby mortar or the rockets invented by Henry Trengrouse and John Dennett. The trials concluded decisively that the rockets were more effective and from that time became the standard equipment in saving life from shipwrecks.

Tom's report on the successful trials persuaded the Board that he should be part of a committee, which was to draw up the *Coastguard Instructions*, published in 1829. Though these *Instructions* stressed the importance of controlling smuggling it is noticeable that the paragraphs about lifesaving bear a remarkable similarity to Sir Thomas Hardy's speech at Tom's wedding.

In 1835 the Verneys moved to London where Tom was appointed to a minor administrative position for the Customs Board. Within two year he had been co-opted onto the Board itself, becoming chairman in 1855. Two years later Queen Victoria knighted him.

Sir Thomas and Lady Perle Verney lived happily in London for the remainder of their lives.

Historical Note

All the characters in this book are fictional except for Admiral Hardy, whose career I have tried to use as accurately as possible, and Colonel James Frampton. Frampton was without doubt an uncompromising soldier and magistrate and it was he who in 1833 sentenced the Tolpuddle Martyrs to transportation to Australia. However his contribution to the founding of the Dorset Yeomanry is still remembered in the county

The four smuggling pubs mentioned, The Cove House Inn at Chiswell, The Lugger in Chickerell, The Black Dog in Weymouth and The Smugglers Inn at Osmington Mills all exist and are worth visiting. Tom's cottage in Brandy Lane, Chesilton (Chiswell) was partially destroyed by the flood of 1979. It remains as a ruin.

Portland Castle is owned by English Heritage and is open to the public. Tout's Quarry on Portland, where Tom and Overton met, is an open-air sculpture park and an excellent place for children to scramble and explore.

The smugglers path from Ringstead Beach to the top of White Nothe makes for an exciting walk though the author has twice managed to lose himself in the brambles of the Undercliff. It was this path that John Meade Falkner describes so vividly in his book *Moonfleet* where he calls it The Zigzag. Thomas Hardy (the author not the sailor) wrote about a smuggling expedition at Ringstead in one of his *Wessex Tales* called *The Distracted Preacher*.

Glossary

The Service	The Coast Guard Service
The Trade	smuggling from *Free Traders*
King's mark	stamp on imported goods to show that duty has been paid
Preventy	local name for a Customs officer from name *Preventive Waterguard*
Gobbler	slang for a Customs Officer
The Bill	Portland Bill
Owlers	local name for smugglers
Brown Bess	nickname for standard British army musket
mobcap	cotton cap worn by women
bunce	slang for an unexpected piece of good fortune
auberge	French inn
georges	colloquial name for sovereigns
seine	fishing net
half-anker	barrel containing 4 gallons
spanker	gaff-rigged sail (fore and aft) on a brigantine
binnacle	housing for a compass on board a ship

Made in the USA
Charleston, SC
23 April 2015